Incubus Tales
A Thousand Words

by Hushicho

Circlet Press, Inc.
Cambridge, MA

Incubus Tales: A Thousand Words
by Hushicho

Print ISBN: 978-1-61390-107-6
Electronic ISBN: 978-1-61390-106-9

Copyright © 2014 Circlet Press, Inc.
Cover Art Copyright © 2013 by Hushicho

For catalog, information about our imprints, review copies, and other information, please write to:

Published by:
Circlet Press, Inc.
39 Hurlbut Street
Cambridge, MA 02138

Or visit us online at: http://www.circlet.com

Contents

Foreword

A picture paints a thousand words. Everyone knows that saying. Speaking as someone who deals with both visual art and the written word, I can say that, to some extent, it is true. There are things I could convey in a single comic panel that would take pages to discuss. On the other hand, there are some things I could present through weaving words that are almost impossible to convey with a visual art; they require painting one's images through the mind's eye.

Doing that is perhaps one of the most exciting forms of art. It is participatory, directly involving the reader in the adventure being written. The author coaxes the reader into the world created, with the characters and events around them, which they must illustrate themselves. All of the senses dip into the world created. Writing can be one of the most sensual acts in the world. Where else is it possible to be so intimate with a person one has never met and indeed may never meet?

Speaking of intimate, speaking of sensual, there is Dhiar, the Incubus, the shopkeeper of Phantasies, and the hero of Incubus Tales. He's older than he looks. Older than almost anyone imagines him to be. He's so optimistic, so hopeful... sometimes I wonder where he came from. Years ago, when I first conceived of him, it was in part because one always sees the Succubus in stories, but almost never the Incubus; if the Incubus is seen, he's made out to be monstrous and unattractive, unappealing. Why should that be so?

And all this business about stealing life-force—that's just silly. But considering the source of so much of this lore, it's unsurprising. They weren't exactly the types to celebrate sex and sensuality, certainly not the types to embrace pleasure and any sort of attitude approaching hedonism.

Dhiar is, though. He's kind and warm, he knows what his lovers want, and he can be everything needed to fulfil those needs.

So considering the origins of the bad PR affecting so many beings like him, why don't we just set the negative aside and try to see him in a more positive light? He's a perfect lover, a fantasy come real in arm's reach.

Like all of us, he has his good days and his bad. It isn't all smooth sailing, but it never is for any of us. Even the perfect lover has many who come into his life and leave it almost as quickly. When eternity is one's playground, every day seems to pass quickly enough. That doesn't make them less significant; if anything, it makes them all the more precious. Perhaps it's better, however, to look at the nights for an Incubus.

In the subterranean cities that he runs between, there's a sense of palpable, tangible darkness. Yet that darkness also has something of a bad rap, an unfair reputation; darkness can be warm and comforting. Darkness can clothe and hold close and protect. Darkness can shut out everything else and give one the feeling that this is the whole world, their whole world. There are long shadows and moments of incredible brilliance intermittently dotting them.

I've named the chapters 'nights', accordingly. It felt appropriate. I also decided to be a little cheeky and use a song reference for each chapter, which means that there are no less than 50 songs for you to see if you can place and recognise. They're all appropriate for listening to their individual chapter, since I did the same when writing. It may give you some idea of my musical tastes, and of course those may very well be quite different to your own, but you might also find yourself turned on to some new tunes.

It is my sincerest hope that *A Thousand Words* will bring you happiness, pleasure, and fulfilment. I also hope, so very much, that what I have written may even open your eyes to some new ideas, some new interests, or at the very least convey why some love them so much. I love to play with sensual ideas, and one of the most exciting and fascinating things is to take something and analyse why someone enjoys it, then try to help others to understand its appeal. It's a challenge, but it's also a unique delight.

Please look upon this as a chronicle of a year in my life and a year or more in Dhiar's. Let's go hand-in-hand into this world of magic and romance and sultry intimacy. Here there are no malefic secrets, only hidden delights. Step forward with me, and without fear or shame, to accept the embrace of the Incubus.

Hushicho
February 2014

1st Night
Dhiar est Amoureux

"Uhh! Yes! *Yes!*"

The bedsprings made little sound, durably-crafted and well-maintained. They had to be; Incubi always demanded it. "A bad bed," the saying amongst them went, "means never fed."

Dhiar, the Incubus in question on this bed, was in fact enjoying quite a feast. An exceptional figure even for his kind, the form he had chosen was well-built and smooth, with hematite-black hair and eyes of deep, dark garnet.

As a demon, his skin always bore a sort of reddish tint to it. At this moment, however, the hint of pink had deepened to outright rose, his muscles gleaming with a sort of matte sheen as he thrust, again and again, into the other man on the bed.

It always seemed ironic somehow, Dhiar reflected, to fuck the delivery boy. Especially if it's pizza. Something about engaging in a stereotype—or was that archetype?—amused the Incubus. Not that he had ever avoided a liaison for that reason alone; plumbers, delivery boys of all types, stable masters, schoolteachers, bakers, acrobats, mimes, lords (with ladies watching)... he had enjoyed them all. Fucking, being fucked, fondling, stroking, licking, nibbling, sucking, bobbing, quaking with ecstasy, dripping with sweat, muscles flexing, balls bouncing...

His mind worked its way back to the present. This lad turned him on: on the cusp of true manhood, a fit body from running around the city all day, a shaggy haircut and just enough stubble on his chin to make him look a bit roguish. There couldn't be any trimming done, with the peppering of chest hair and the fluffy bush nestling around the base of the erection that slapped against the younger man's body with every motion.

It was likely that, in this city, deliveries were planned with at least an hour's destination time in-between, even if they were next door to each other. If he had not decided to open Phantasies, Dhiar mused, he would have been a delivery boy. There was no end to the variety of people, from one area to another. Boroughs, levels, circles... it largely depended on who told the story as to the specific term used. Even those of the same kind or in the same area were not necessarily similar. Even those of the same blood, the same lineage, the same line might not remotely resemble each other. It was exhilarating.

Noctemburg gripped Dhiar, compelled his joie de vivre. It was here that his shop Phantasies first opened its doors. It was here he felt so completely at home. And, though not particularly a city one might consider safe or secure, it nonetheless felt like home.

Its cavernous spread lay beneath the surface of the Earth, beneath the streets that mundane humans walked and considered themselves masters of, beneath their notice and yet so far beyond anything most of them could imagine. The spires of the taller buildings stretched up, falling short of the ceiling. It loomed over the city like a protective dome, and Noctemburg stretched for miles in every direction.

Naturally, doorways led to and from the surface world. Trains even ran between the two places. It wasn't a matter of being secret, or invisible, or any of those things. It was a matter of being completely pedestrian about everything, which made the dullards believe there was nothing at all noteworthy about the sparkling woman with iridescent wings who just ducked in an alcove and vanished completely from sight.

Anyone could go to Noctemburg. But only the truly special settled there for any length of time.

A series of moans vibrated up from the delivery boy's chest, dipping dangerously into the realm of whining, his stomach coated with the thick, white proof of his excitement. Dhiar slid out with a shiver, gasping as he managed to add to that, a snowy splash on the golden brown hairs between the lad's legs.

"Ooh," the Incubus whispered. "Bonus."

It took remarkably little time for clean-up, and soon Dhiar was alone again in his shop. He didn't bother to put on any clothes. In this city, there were plenty of places where people went in expecting nudity. The shop already boasted a rather large wall of phallic-shaped toys, what was one more penis between friends?

He lounged in the chair behind the counter, half-curled into the capacious space piled with cushions and blankets. Even if temperature shifts meant anything to him, he could wallow naked there indefinitely.

A sigh escaped his lips. The boxes were not putting themselves away. It was really almost enough to make him dread the weekly deliveries, but the sex was too enjoyable. He would have to see if he couldn't put on some of the old Incubus charm and somehow finagle his way into getting the young man to lend him a hand next time.

For that matter, a few of the other fellows had made eyes at him. The Incubus tilted his head back a bit, going over their faces in his memory. He had explored every detail visually. He wondered how long it would take if he really turned on his charm.

Eventually, the thought of having to do it later nagged at Dhiar's mind for long enough. He pushed to his feet and crossed the room, stepping between drapes and shelves and into the back room. This was not the room where he lived—he made his home in the loft upstairs—but it was the place he gave the most of his guests appreciative service.

Accordingly, this was the last place he had seen his clothing. With Dhiar, clothes tended to scatter to the winds whenever anything started. He couldn't always remember where he'd cast them, and naturally he couldn't be expected to know where they might fall after they left contact with his skin. If rushed, he made a kind of spectacle, clothes exploding off in every direction.

"Ah! There we go."

It was a start. He tugged his boxer shorts on, the black ones with little cartoony red devils. They had so amused him when he saw them in the catalogue. Little red devils, that's what humanity assumed he was.

He got the attitude right, for one.

2nd Night
Your Disco Needs You

The music thumped at a steady beat. This wasn't the kind of club where you felt it, though, instead of hearing it. The words lingered in the air and the minds of the dancers, the musical accompaniment managing to be more than just background noise. This was a good band, a good club.

The dancers on the floor all moved like they knew how. Each and every one of them writhed with confidence, their forms animated by the stimulus of love, desire, and loss chronicled in the unfurling song around them all. It gave them something in common, when nothing else managed: this common ground, this common song, the sweat moistening the air.

As the last lingering strains of electric guitar faded, Dhiar was already halfway to the bar. He slipped onto a stool, leaning his arms onto the bar's surface.

"A glass of water and a raspberry daiquiri, please." The Incubus called politely, if firmly, to the man behind all of the glasses and napkin holders.

Dhiar ran his fingers through his hair, but those hematite-black curls bounced all around and into much the same places as they had been before. To have done so much, so furiously pushed his body for so long, he barely shimmered with the glow of perspiration. He suspected that his desires for water merely imitated the actual need for it, because of his constant dallying with humans.

Perhaps, he reflected, it was their dallying with him.

Either way, he felt parched. But as he twisted around on the stool's seat once more, his eyes caught on a lad, surely no older than twenty, hair wild and thick and a spectrum of colours. His left eyebrow sported three piercings, on his lower lip a single spike jutting out underneath. Normally Dhiar would not have given him a second glance, but this time, this time...

Something was different about him. He seemed entirely unlike the type most would presume. The piercings actually worked, for one. They accented his looks, rather than managed to be the entirety of his allure.

Before the bartender could go to him, Dhiar snatched the man's sleeve and whispered into his ear.

Maybe it was a cliché, he didn't care. Buying drinks usually led to conversation, or at least a look. And when one is an Incubus, a look is all that is needed...

Beer! He got a bottle of beer! A grin crossed the young man's face as he lifted it in Dhiar's direction, a sort of salute. Dhiar, in return, raised his drink and then nodded his head back, beckoning casually. His eyes sparkled, looking distinctly luminous in the darkened club full of strobes and coloured laser lights.

"Hey."

Dhiar tried not to shiver obviously. This boy's voice was sweet and rough at the same time, probably sweet naturally and rough from the cigarettes he could smell. They weren't cheap cigarettes, not by any means. Not what one might expect. "Hey. Enjoying yourself tonight?"

"Even more now that I'm getting free drinks! I'm Evvin, what do they call you?"

The Incubus grinned at once. "Dhiar." He extended his hand to take Evvin's, squeezing it and then releasing it. He fought his urge to kiss it. "I'm sure I've not seen you here before, and I come here pretty often. Is this your first time?"

"Ooh." Evvin caught the little double-entendre, leaning closer. Even with the rest of the ambient scents in the room, mostly fresh sweat and arousal all around the dance floor, Dhiar could smell him. It was a delicious scent, delightful, masculine... he could smell interest, piquant and insouciant. "I guess you could say that. I got bored just hanging around the clubs uptown. It's all kinda..."

"Hoity-toity," Dhiar offered.

"Yeah!" Evvin started to laugh, leaning sidelong against the bar. "That's exactly what it is! Especially Angel-town."

The Incubus made a sour face. It wasn't that he had anything to do with angels, especially not in the way that most might assume. Demons and angels weren't opposites, or working for opposing teams by default. Some of them clashed, of course, because angels were messengers, sometimes free agents and sometimes engaged by certain beings, and demons were ever free agents, fiercely independent and following their own joy.

Angel-town was the part of the city that was a sort of ghetto for the more high-minded of the angels. Although there were plenty of them who comported themselves with the dignity of independent messengers—as they more or less all were, in Noctemburg—there were a distinct and influential few who marred the experience by furthering the stereotypes and making it a point to be elitist, and especially unkind to demons.

"You won't find any of that here." Dhiar set his glass down after another sip from it. "I have a little shop not far from here. Phantasies. Have you been yet? You might like it... it's definitely nothing you'd find in Angel-town!"

"Really! Well..." Evvin took another gulp of his beer. "Why don't you lead the way? I think my drink's portable enough."

The Incubus needed no further invitation. Finishing as much of his daiquiri as possible, he set the glass on the bar and tossed a wave to the bartender, walking for the door without looking back. Either he'd be followed, or he wouldn't. He was beyond the Orpheus Syndrome leaving clubs. He no longer had time for that kind of game.

Fingers, a bit clammy from holding a frosty bottle, found his hand and wove with his own fingers. Dhiar turned his head to see Evvin, looking sheepish, boyish really, swinging his hand in the demon's. No words were exchanged. They didn't need to be.

The streets were all but deserted, aside from the occasional milling of pedestrians up and down in the darkness. Noctemburg never really had a "day" to speak of, being underground as the city was. But it was currently in the cycle commonly regarded as night. A Wednesday night. Who goes out on a Wednesday? Besides himself, the Incubus could only think of...the gorgeous man holding his hand and sipping a beer, walking along beside him.

He took in a slow breath, closing his eyes for a moment and then opening them again, half-expecting Evvin to have vanished, just a dream or a hallucination or some side-effect of drinking. But, as if reading his thoughts, Evvin squeezed his hand, grinning again to him. It was an encouraging gesture, unquestionably affectionate.

Dhiar stopped himself, turning his head the other way. "Oh... oh! Here we are!"

The neon sign reading "Phantasies" glowed in cherry-red through the darkness, the lights inside turned down and the sign on the door reading "Gone out—back in a bit!"

Stepping to the door, Dhiar simply reached out and pushed. It swung inward, and he glanced over his shoulder, pulling the other man inside by his hand. "Here we are," he called back. "Home sweet home!"

3rd Night
Feel It

They had enjoyed drinks together at the club. The only thing left over was an empty beer bottle, rested on the counter beside the register. No need for fresh drinks. Their thirst had found other means.

It was cold outside. It was always fairly cool, being subterranean, but sometimes certain features of the city—and of course, stray magic residue—led to variation in temperature, however subtle. The most delightful thing about Noctemburg's unique weather, in Dhiar's mind, was the fact that it could and did rain, thanks to underground water sources and natural condensation. At certain times of the year, mist blanketed city streets like spun cotton. He felt like he was crawling in bedclothes, when he went out on those days.

There was snow, too, and ice. Even sometimes against the expectations of anyone, weather happened. As irrepressibly as inconvenient family members dropping by, it persisted. He suspected that it had not so much begun by the mysterious forces of nature as simply manifested due to massive conflicting sorceries.

Right then it had begun to rain, and when it rained in Noctemburg, it poured.

"Just in time!" Evvin laughed, looking out the tinted glass door to the street. "Wow. It's really coming down."

Something about narrowly missing the downpour excited Dhiar, even though it nagged at him with a little regret. He loved the rain, loved it with a passion. With a moment's hesitation, and only that moment's, he reached his hand out and laced his fingers in Evvin's. No words passed between them. He pulled open the door, looked over his shoulder into the young man's eyes, and tugged him out into the street, out from under the eaves, into the torrential pour of water.

Two sets of eyes met, electric, melting into each other's vision. Suddenly they were so close, and then suddenly they had both closed their eyes, bodies together, soaking wet, sodden clothes clinging to their forms. Evvin could swear he felt a spark between their lips as they met, salty and sweet, from the rain and the remaining alcohol left over in their mouths. He tasted the robust flavour of fermented wheat, tempered by Incubus delights.

Their tongues met in the middle and wrestled for a moment, barely more than a twinkling. In Dhiar's experience, less was always more in this respect. He had once coined the term 'slug-wrestling' to describe less capable kisses. With the scantest touch, sparing and rare, it became more exciting.

Not that he wasn't amused by the earnest efforts of the inexperienced. Quite the opposite, their eagerness and fervour, that rare and intense heat, tickled him from the pit of his stomach. But everyone had to learn sometime, and so he eased them along the path of the skilled.

The lips first must massage, he decided, must explore each other and contact each other. Breath is shared and, in a way, life. One of the most intimate things was sharing breath, even a little. What other things could dive so deeply into one person, to emerge with a report from inside them? And so quickly, so easy to miss, like that often-mentioned thief in the night.

The teeth part. The tongue longs to explore, to lick the back of another set of teeth. It longs for the contact that it only ever receives from food and drink.

Amid the rushing of the water around and upon them, between them, they both moaned at the same time. Their eyes opened, and each looked upon the other's face. The rain ate the sound, but the resonant vibrations remained. The vibrations, noises made, they could penetrate so deeply into another too.

Dhiar curled his hips forward, barely pressing his hips against Evvin's, and then suddenly there came an audible cry, even above the downpour. He looked hastily down, hiding his eyes from the Incubus, and tried to mouth something too quiet. But Dhiar knew all too well what had happened. A puckish grin curled along his lips.

He didn't have to have it happen inside his body, or against bare flesh. That it happened was reward enough for him. Reaching out again, he wrapped his fingers around Evvin's wrist and led him back in, standing both of them on the wide welcome mat.

"Let's get out of these wet clothes," Dhiar suggested, reaching over to roll Evvin's shirt up his body. "I wouldn't want you to catch cold."

Pale from the wetness and rose-tinted from his embarrassment, Evvin could only stand and do as he was positioned, losing his clothes above the waist quickly. He scrambled to keep his pants up as Dhiar's fingers unfastened his buttons offhand.

"W-wait!" He stammered, clearing his throat and at last looking into Dhiar's eyes again. "I... uh... I can explain..."

Dhiar leaned closer, his breath still warm and fresh, his eyes deep and clear. "No need," he murmured in confidential tones. "I'm an Incubus. You lasted much longer than most, you know."

"I... I did?"

"You did!" Dhiar batted the hands away and worked the clingy fabric down to Evvin's ankles, then did the same with his transparent boxer shorts. The electric blue hid absolutely nothing. It might as well have been tissue paper. "Usually we meet in a bar or something like that, or a club, we get halfway home, then they get horny. The first real intimate touch, or the first kiss... they've lost it. It's gone." He flashed a toothy grin, tugging Evvin's boots off and helping him to step out of the rest of his clothing.

"So... so it's always that intense?"

"It's a gift of mine," Dhiar explained, reaching up to stroke the sensitive skin, carefully so he didn't cause any discomfort. "I share with you the sensations that I feel, and the sensations that I feel from you. So it forms an intense feedback loop that can be extremely fulfilling and rewarding, but it does take some getting used to."

Evvin could not help himself, as he felt his penis rise and fill. He leaned back against the cool glass of the door, a shiver coursing along his back. His lush buttocks pressed against the pane. Anyone walking by who could see through the heavy rain would get quite a show.

Dhiar harbored love in his eyes as he gazed before him, his fingers slowly rolling Evvin's balls, from one to the other. "Just say when. We've got a nice, long, mouth-watering night ahead of us."

4th Night
A Case of You

Dhiar wished he smoked. He could start, he knew, but he didn't really want to. It's not that he had any concerns for his body—he could manipulate every part of it, if need be—but he simply didn't like the taste.

Incense was a different thing altogether. His fingers slipped into the little paper wrapper and pulled out a stalk, setting it in its holder. The box of matches made rushing sounds like a rain stick when he picked it up. He clasped a single wooden match with his fingernails and drew it out, holding it more firmly to strike it, and then to light the tip of the incense.

The end grew cherry-red as he blew on it. Fragrant smoke, faintly kissed with rose's perfume, curled into the air. No sound came but the sound of the matchbox being set softly down again.

The demon's dark garnet eyes followed the twists and winding of the wisps of smoke. It lulled him to relaxation. He didn't need to sleep, or else he'd be unconscious with the gorgeous thing he had brought home. Right now, more than anything, he needed to be awake. He needed to think.

Breath rushed cool over his lips and back out again, warmer than it had come. He barely blinked. His shoulders rose and fell slowly, so slowly that any observers might mistake him for a statue or for furniture.

It never got too bright in Noctemburg. But it was never darker than when the soul was dark as well, when the heart was burdened and the memory too keen. The Incubus let his head tilt slowly to the right, his inner voice playing a wistful song he had heard once, a long time ago, at a place far from that room.

The thing about songs, he reflected inwardly, is that they're so easy to laugh at and so easy to poke fun at by changing words or exaggerating. Despite all this, the actual song is the one that always sticks in your mind. Just when you thought you've forgotten, you hear something that reminds you vaguely of the melody and suddenly you're singing along, backwards and forwards. You can escape anything, he mused, but a song.

It was the blond hair and the blue eyes that always got to him. He could see them as clear as... well, as clear as what passed for day in Noctemburg. As clear as when he stood in a well-lit room. The sad look gazing from the platform as the train arrived, and then he had to admit his vision faltered for lack of clarity. Excess moisture always ruined that.

Dee... it hadn't been good. The whole thing wouldn't work, he could've told the man that from the start. They were both nocturnal, at least. One thing in common. Everything else seemed cast in diametric opposite. They had shared moments of brilliant resonance, moments of passion and desire, moments of romantic love and affection, and just as many moments of contention, clashing, and distaste.

The bad always tended to fade, whether for the mind's own protection from the pain, or from a simple lack of desire to retain unpleasant memories. It led to sentimentality. Sometimes it led to foolish resuming.

He knew he would never lose the feelings that he still had for Dee. He'd heard a story once, about a grandfather and his grandson, who sat down together, and each showed the other his heart: the grandson's was pure and unblemished and as a heart always appeared in the loveliest of valentines, whereas the grandfather's was a mass of patchwork with pieces that didn't fit the holes and weren't the right shape, colour, or texture.

When the boy asked his grandfather why it was like that, and didn't it hurt, the grandfather answered that it did hurt sometimes, but the good feelings outweighed the bad. That every time he met someone and cared for someone, he would pinch a piece of his heart and give it to them, and they did it for him too. And even if they ended up parting ways, those pieces of heart could never be returned. They could never go back.

At the end, touched, the grandson pinched off a piece of his heart and offered it to his grandfather, and his grandfather did the same in return.

The song in his head had mentioned something about love being when two souls touch. He could believe that. Souls, like fine wines, mingling inextricably. If even for a moment, they would forever bear the taste of the other.

Dhiar stretched his arms over his head and walked to the window, naked, comfortable in his skin. He had worked hard to sculpt this body through will to what he decided to make it. All of his brethren were the same. Most of them stayed true to their favourite form and barely changed it throughout their existences. Even small changes took sometimes years or longer to decide.

He ran his hand over his chest, down over his stomach, letting his hand fall to the side, fingertips brushing through the soft black hairs sparkling between his legs. No Moon smiled down on Noctemburg aside from the one someone had grandiosely painted on the tall canopy of rock; who knows how they got up there to do it. But the lights of the city managed to make a persistent glow.

The scent of roses hanging faintly in the air soothed him. He barely started as he felt a hand touch his shoulder.

"Hey," Evvin croaked, voice rough and filled with sleep. "Extended bathroom break?"

Dhiar reached up to place his hand upon Evvin's. "No, just... well, I don't actually have to sleep, except for a little rest every few weeks. I figured I'd spare you my tossing and turning."

The other man slipped his hand back and then wrapped his arms around the Incubus from behind, pressing up against him, rubbing up against his backside. He linked his hands in front, around Dhiar's waist.

"What time is it?"

"Does it matter?"

Evvin laughed at that quick response. "I guess not. You gonna fix me breakfast before you send me on my way?"

"Tsk." Dhiar turned and reached up, cupping Evvin's cheeks

with his hands and looking deep, deep into his eyes. "I am not going to send you on your way. You can stay here today... a week... forever, whatever. I'm not going to turn you out just because we slept together, you know."

"Really?" Evvin stretched his fingers out and rubbed at the top of the Incubus's buttocks. "I could abuse that."

Dhiar patted Evvin's cheek and then let his arms rest upon the man's shoulders. "But if you opt for the 'forever' one, I'm going to have to require your assistance in the shop. You can at least lounge around on the sales floor and look pretty."

Laughter again rose in the room, floating and lingering with the rose fragrance.

5th Night
Get to Burning

"You're an amazing cook, Dhiar!" Evvin rubbed his full stomach, smiling appreciatively to the Incubus seated next to him.

In front of them, on the coffee table in the centre of the sofa and chairs, sat a clay pot, and in it rested the meagre remains of the broth and fragments of food. The room still bore the comforting aroma of kabocha and tofu.

Dhiar slid his arms around Evvin's shoulders with a pleased purr, a rumble of sound in his throat as he began to speak. "This? This was just a simple dish. Surely anyone could make it at least as well. But I'm glad you liked it."

"Well, my grandmother makes this sometimes." Evvin reached out and dipped a finger in the remaining broth, then sucked his finger dry. "Mm. And she's pretty old."

Dhiar's lips curled into a knowing grin. "I've already put a few centuries behind me. I guess not everyone concentrates on cooking, though. I just... think it's an important and simple pleasure." His hand dropped to Evvin's chest, stroking in circles through the sleeveless red shirt he wore indoors. "I don't have to eat human food, but it's awfully nice."

"Mm." Evvin turned his head, cupping Dhiar's cheek with his warm, slightly wet hand. "I know what you like."

"You certainly do!"

The Incubus tickled his fingertips to the wide armhole and slid in over a smooth chest. It took him a moment, and then...

"Ah!" Evvin's eyes grew wide and his grin toothy and broad as fingers found his pierced nipple. He leaned in and met Dhiar's mouth with his own, reaching back to pull the ribbon that kept the demon's hematite-black hair in a ponytail.

It tumbled down along with the two of them, arms and legs weaving, lips finding each other for a repeat engagement. A little tongue chanced to flick amid the embrace, to be met by another. The rich scent of their dinner was joined, and then overwhelmed, by the smell of arousal.

Dhiar slipped his hand down to Evvin's hip, then around front of his demolished jeans, barely holding together by the grace of some supreme being and a questionable amount of safety pins. As with all clothing, the button and zip practically melted to his touch, falling open easily. The scent became stronger as bare flesh brushed against bare flesh. His lover's finger had dried from broth and spit, but the treasure in those jeans had already grown wet.

"Naughty boy," Dhiar whispered hoarsely, dipping his head to kiss along Evvin's jaw, to the corner. Then he nibbled at the side of his lover's neck, breathing hot against his skin. "So naughty."

The other man made no verbal answer, but instead he firmly reached down and pulled the ties at Dhiar's hips, then tugged the demon's trousers to his ankles. Grinning again as before, he gazed into Dhiar's eyes, reaching his hand down to take both of their lengths in it. A surge of electric pleasure coursed between the two of them, the Incubus gift heightening the sensation and setting the loop of bliss into motion.

Some regarded empathy as a curse, but it had only ever been a blessing as far as Dhiar was concerned. He could feel all of the sensations running through Evvin as if they were his own, and he could feed, in turn, those feelings and his own back through his lover... and they would come back, only to return in the cycle and increase every time.

The first time, Evvin lasted an impressive thirty seconds. By now, he craved that burst of stimulation. His muscles pulsed in anticipation, his body moist with a thin layer of sweat from the hot dinner and the hotter dessert. His cheeks turned a rosy pink as he heard himself moan into the air. To try and muffle it, he pressed his mouth to Dhiar's.

Hearts beat together, pounding a rhythm of vibrations between the chests pressed against each other. Two bodies rocked at a quickening pace, hot breaths between them, between the bridges each kiss made. Sweat and sex, sweet and strong, rose around them.

"I'm..." Evvin started, but rather than speak another word, he ended up crying out.

What he was doing became all too apparent as it became very hot and very sticky between the two men's bodies. Electric sparkles swam before Evvin's eyes as the bushy-haired man's jaw dropped, overcome entirely by the flood of ecstasy running over his body. He could feel his hand covered with his own seed, then with Dhiar's, as it added to the amount. So quick. So brief. His cheeks burned with a kind of shame, even amid the delight, for being unable to hold on any longer.

When he opened his eyes, he hesitated for a moment before looking up. Then he smiled, meeting Dhiar's warm eyes, his gentle smile. "That was so good."

"Really?" Evvin squeezed his hand around the both of them, down under, drawing in a sudden hiss of breath as the ill-considered gesture sent its shock of oversensitive stimulation up his back. "I'm er... sorry we've not... you know... inside, or..."

"Usually it takes most people a few tries. And that takes a few days." Dhiar leaned up, kissing the very tip of Evvin's nose. "We have forever. I'm not that concerned."

"Forever..."

"Forever. So don't worry too much." Dhiar slid his hands up along the soft curve of the other man's buttocks, grabbing two handfuls. "We have all the time you need. Now..." His eyes gleamed with their usual mischievous energy. "Were you going to wipe that up, or would you like to just keep going as-is until we need to go continue in the bath?"

The bath! Evvin's heart leapt at the thought. It was so welcoming, full of plants and that huge garden tub... the skylight, the feeling of being a bit exposed, the dizzying bath salts, all of it...

"The bath then, is it?" Dhiar raised his eyebrows momentarily, snatching a kiss. "I can see the gears turning in your mind."

Had he employed some kind of telepathy? Evvin felt even naughtier at that thought. He absently returned the kiss, then tucked his face along the side of Dhiar's neck, kissing it a handful of times.

"Let's go in the bath," Evvin murmured, muffled just a tad.

6th Night
La La La

Was this what made a kept man? Evvin arranged the elegant glass phials of oil on the shelf. His mind was never entirely on work like this. Either Dhiar distracted him, or something else did. Tedious work never kept his concentration long. Still, the atmosphere of Phantasies calmed his mind and made it easier. He could appreciate the pleasant qualities effortlessly now.

He was dressed better than he had ever been, fed better than he had ever been... still a bit bony, he had gained some weight. But Dhiar only fawned over him more. It wasn't like this with the humans in the city, or the vampires for example. It was easy to criticise someone for being heavier than you when you don't actually have to eat food.

Evvin snorted to himself with amusement, lips curling into a grin. The glass containers clinked as he slid them back together.

His breath caught in his throat as the sound of chimes at the door fluttered to his ears. He wasn't ready for this! Come on Dhiar, he thought, hurry back! It can't take that long to get groceries!

Summoning up all his courage and calm, Evvin stepped out from the shelf, offering a stiff wave in the direction of the door. "Welcome to Phantasies!" He called out, wearing a grin that looked more than anything like a comical imitation of Dhiar.

There, at the door, stood a redhead in a verdant green catsuit, open to just below the waist, sleeveless and complemented by a white belt about the hips and sleek boots of the same colour. Her eyes were green too, and her figure immaculate. She didn't really resemble their usual clientèle, especially in this part of the city, but as long as she refrained from propositioning him, Evvin felt confident enough in his ability.

"Dhiar?"

Evvin's mouth opened, but before words could come out of it, she was there with her arms around him.

"Oh Dhi-Dhi, it's been so long!" After a moment, the woman gasped and released her hold. "I'm so sorry! What am I thinking? You like boys..."

Really, Evvin thought, I ought to say something.

But his vocal chords seemed not to be functioning properly. As he struggled with speaking, she spun around in place. He couldn't trace the movement, it was so quick. When she stopped, turning to him, he noticed that this redhead had somehow become male, hair shorter, a little stubble on his chin, ginger hairs across the exposed skin of his chest.

"Sorry," the redhead continued, flinging his arms around Evvin again. "Oh, you remember my twin, right?"

Suddenly there was another redhead standing there, almost like a carbon copy of the first, identical except that his hair seemed to be parted on the opposite side.

Evvin's mind raced. How could he concentrate like this? Must think of Dhiar; he tried to centre his mind. What would Dhiar do in a situation like this? Oh, it felt so good. He wondered if they were Incubi like Dhiar. It all threatened to overwhelm him.

"I... I'm not Dhiar!" He managed, just barely, voice cracking.

The twins gasped as one and stepped back, releasing him. The second tilted his head to the side, scrutinising the flustered boy. Then his hand went to his mouth, which hung open in surprise.

"Oh my! You're not!"

The first, however, started to giggle, shaking his head. "Well, look at us! We did say it had been a long time."

"It's okay." Evvin ran a hand through his rainbow of hair, ruffling it to calm himself. He had forced his breath slower, coming down from the contact high of pleasure. "So you two... Incubi? Or like... Succubi?" He had heard a little from Dhiar about how that worked, but the exact terminology was beyond him.

"Lydia," the first redhead offered, smiling as he held out his hand.

The second chimed in, "Lydie!"

As Evvin took Lydia's hand and shook it, they both spoke at exactly the same time. "The term isn't important, just the pleasure!"

They both laughed, and Evvin joined in despite himself. "Sorry. I don't know much about this. All I know is Dhiar, and not much about him."

Lydia draped his arms around his twin's shoulders, leaning their heads together. "We could tell you, if you want to know."

"If you want," Lydie echoed, reaching out a finger to trace down Evvin's chest.

It occurred to Evvin that they were a lot like Dhiar, in that they seemed completely unhesitant to seduce him. Yet at the same time, they were not so much like Dhiar, because the charming shopkeeper was much more subtle. Older, perhaps? He couldn't tell. It made little difference. From what he knew, Incubi could alter their appearances at will. But something about them seemed "young", not quite so experienced as his lover.

And his lover... would Dhiar be jealous if he came in to find the twins with their hands on Evvin? Would this all turn into an unpleasant situation? Dhiar didn't seem like the jealous type, but he unquestionably had his sensitive moments.

"I... um, I think we should have tea and wait for Dhiar." Evvin forced a weak smile that threatened to collapse under its own meagre weight at any moment. "So he can enjoy this! You two seem like really great guys." He nibbled his lower lip. "Gals. What... whatever?"

The twins started to laugh again, looking to each other, then the young man before them. "We are what we are, whenever we are that," Lydie began. "You don't have to feel self-conscious," Lydia chimed in. It was as if they shared the same mind.

Suddenly the door opened, filling the room with sound. Evvin released a sigh of relief.

"Lydia! Lydie!" Dhiar set his box of groceries in the seat of the chair next to the door, then he opened his arms wide. "It's been so long!"

The two redheads leapt to Dhiar, laughing as they hugged him in their arms, kissing his face and keeping close. The three of them looked so happy together.

Evvin shook his head, hooking his thumbs in his pockets idly. He forced himself to move, walking towards the tea shelf. "I'll fix us some tea, like you like. You three can catch up!"

"Mm, let me help you!" Dhiar squeezed Lydia and Lydie, waving them towards the counter to sit, then jogging to catch Evvin up. He leaned in to kiss the curve of his lover's ear, dropping his voice. "Sorry it took so long," he murmured. "You never cease to amaze me. Such restraint! But you don't have to. If it were me, I'd have been in the middle of a twin sandwich by now!"

Evvin laughed a little louder than he meant to, turning his head to catch Dhiar's lips with a genuine and grateful kiss. If only the Incubus knew...!

7th Night
Polite Dance Song

Dhiar sipped at a mixed drink, full of sweetness and fruit. He could barely even taste the alcohol, which was the best way to have it; no-one except a real alcoholic—or a connoisseur, as the term tended to be softened—actually wanted to taste the booze. It was all the same to him, tasting it or not tasting it, but on the whole he preferred the fruity bouquet. He had a sweet tooth, and fruit satisfied it much more perfectly than most confection.

The festivities were nothing short of marvellous. It was one of the many and frequent holidays celebrated in the city, and some of the vampires had decided to throw a ball for it. Obscure holiday, much like the Yuletide in sentiment and decking, and so Dhiar had thrown on a green and red ensemble, mostly crushed velvet and dainty foppish fare.

Evvin would regret not having come along, after the Incubus told him about it. So far, there had been massive amounts of sex even before the first actual break in the orchestra's set. It was a chamber orchestra, all curiously (and somewhat conspicuously) boasting a kind of unsettling normalcy. It was perfectly conceivable that they might actually just be boring humans, but Dhiar suspected that, sooner or later, one would sprout tentacles from her throat or reveal that he had six penises, or something of that sort.

And speaking of penises, Dhiar found his eyes attracted to a blond man conveniently framing his with a hand rubbing along his thigh. My, my. Undoubtedly a vampire, and undoubtedly one that had to be careful with his blood supply concentrating itself in entirely the wrong regions of his body.

Within three minutes, the two were entangled in a side parlour, stumbling over the love sofa and then rolling lightly upon it, a leg curled around a waist, a hand sliding up over a shoulder. Even the hairs on Dhiar's body responded to the stimulus, raising goose-flesh with all of the kisses, the licks...

"Now hold on a moment!" The Incubus frowned and shoved back at the vampire's face.

The blond steepled his eyebrows, a puzzled expression crossing his features.

"You can't do that," Dhiar continued, huffing as he folded his arms over his chest. This was not particularly an easy accomplishment with another man draped over him like a blanket, but somehow he managed it. "I'm a demon. Do you know how potent demon blood is? Not that I'd be particularly offended if you tried to suck me," he wiggled his eyebrows, "and I mean that in any sense, but you'd be bouncing off the walls if you didn't burn your little mind out like a sparkler."

For a few seconds, the vampire stared, and then his brows lowered. "Is that true, or are you really just unfond of..." He motioned to himself.

"Me?" Dhiar started to laugh, unfolding his arms and wrapping them around the blond undead atop him. "No, I quite like vampires. You're so dandy and inexorable. No, I don't have anything against you. I just didn't want you to be overwhelmed by sensation. I'm an Incubus, you see... you take a sip of my vitae, so to speak, and you'd be getting bursts of every orgasm in a mile."

"Every...?"

"And you'd be constantly aroused until you worked it out of your system, and with what I was seeing in the ballroom, well..."

"Ah." The vampire adopted what could only be called a sheepish grin. It was clearly one of the first times he had ever worn such an expression. "Well, if you'd like to still... you know..."

"Mm?"

"Well I mean," the blond man leaned closer to Dhiar, "I don't know if I'll ever get the opportunity again. To do this with a real Incubus."

"It's not that rare," Dhiar casually waved his hand, then replaced it to caress along his clumsy lover's shoulder. "I run a shop a few levels down... it's called Phantasies, you can't miss it. Literally the only shop of its kind."

The vampire slowly nodded his head, thoughtful as he drew his tongue over his lips, dampening them. "Well then, I shall have to—"

He trailed off as it became clear Dhiar's hands were not both on his back, and in fact one was sliding beyond his waistband, moving the tucked shirt out of the way and groping outright through the silk shorts that only barely sheathed the sizeable shaft behind them.

Dhiar glanced up at the sudden quiet. "Hmm? Oh, sorry. Did I interrupt you? Maybe we should take our clothes off so we aren't distracted by the whole getting-past-clothing strategy."

"Er."

The Incubus didn't hesitate. Even if externally the vampire hesitated and looked completely surprised by the invitation, he knew this sort of situation all too well. Moving quickly, the clothes were worked aside, to reveal pale, muscular, slender skin. Clumsier hands attempted to tug at the fine crushed velvet on Dhiar's body, and his own talents helped those hands to undress him. Soon, two naked bodies rubbed slowly against each other.

Dhiar lifted his lips, to catch the vampire's, nuzzling at him, nipping his lower lip and then kissing at the corner of his mouth, at the side, slowly working his way back to press mouth to mouth.

It was actually rather special to him. His partner had managed to last this long. Most of them didn't last past the first touch below the waist. But he could also tell that it wouldn't be very long at all before it all stumbled over the edge. How sweet it would be! He didn't care. He kept kissing, lifting his hips to smack his erection against the vampire's pulsing rod. He would need a little sip of blood after their fun, Dhiar knew. Oh well, he didn't mind. It wasn't as if they were going to drink it all!

He giggled to himself, thinking about this impressionable young vampire receiving the impulses of pleasure from the other party guests. With his endowment, he would be able to find promising work as a weathervane for a week.

"I think," Dhiar murmured, "I'm going to enjoy this."

8th Night
Edge

"Evvin, you look so cute in glasses."

The words from Dhiar took Evvin by surprise, and his cheeks turned a slight pink. "Thanks... um..." He quietly pulled his solid black glasses off, sliding them into the soft case and setting it aside.

Addressing the unspoken question, Dhiar motioned with a flourish of the wrist to the handsome blond man beside him. Handsome, and very pale.

"This is Baron Anton Hauser. I hope you'll make him welcome." Leaning closer, the Incubus lowered his voice to a stage whisper, easily audible by everyone in the room. "He's a vampire, you know!"

Anton smirked, inclining his head in respectful acknowledgement of both the fact and his new acquaintance. "Yes, what Dhiar says is true. We met at the ball... it's a pity you chose not to attend."

"Oh yes! Darling!" Dhiar tossed his arm around Evvin's shoulders, leading him closer to the vampire, for the two to look each other over. "Anton was not the only delight at the party. There was also a chamber orchestra, unlimited champagne, and all kinds of finger foods!" He paused for a moment, pooching his lips in thought, then continued. "Well. Probably not technically, 'unlimited' champagne, considering. But more than most would care to drink."

"I'm pleased to meet you," Anton chimed in, reaching down to take Evvin's hand and shaking it briefly, a single pulse and a squeeze. "Dhiar has told me much about you."

"Well, you know..." The Incubus casually waved his hand, wiggling his fingers. "I had to mention my favourite shopkeeper's assistant!" He gave a wink and bumped his hip against Evvin's.

At first, Evvin had no idea what to make of this. He was totally fine with Dhiar meeting and doing things with other people, but he hadn't expected him to bring them home with him. Still, it seemed impossible to be too tense around Dhiar. Evvin couldn't help himself, and finally let out a breathy laugh.

"Pleased to meet you too, Baron."

"Please, just Anton. No need for formalities."

"Anton," Evvin corrected himself. "So... what's in store? Is Anton staying?"

Dhiar patted both men on the shoulder and walked behind the counter, rummaging beneath it and producing some teacups, to set upon its surface. He kept a whole world under there. "I just wanted him to stop by for a drink. And so he could know where the shop is... I'm going to be giving him some training! And if you'd like, you can help me!"

Evvin almost couldn't help himself. He knew this man, this vampire, was Dhiar's catch, so to speak. But the nature of the vampire, just as the nature of the Incubus, was to draw the eye to them, and all the other senses as well. Even the scent of the man was almost intoxicating. Surely Dhiar knew. But he was probably immune to its effects.

"Oh?" Evvin immediately turned his head, snapped out of his sort of trance. "What... er... what sort of training would that be?"

"Sexual!" Dhiar popped up, all smiles and sparkles in his eyes. "He had a sip of my blood. Hickey, you know." He motioned to his neck, where rapidly-fading twin red marks sat upon the skin. "Anyway, he'll be especially sensitive for probably a few more days... and he asked me to help him... come to terms, with his new sensual awareness."

"What delicate phrasing!" Anton laughed, the kind of sound that sounded manly and youthful at the same time. Every time he moved, he held himself with such noble bearing. It was more than Evvin had ever seen. But at times it was a little stiff, as if he had rarely left the circles of nobility to interact with others.

Maybe he hadn't, Evvin reflected. Maybe the vampire ran primarily in his own circles. Dhiar had said, before leaving to attend the party, that it would be chiefly vampires in attendance. Few others ever bothered, or perhaps dared, to mingle.

Dhiar easily poured the spoonfuls of tea into metal balls, fixing the clasps and putting each one into a cup. "Naturally! I'm a delicate speaker," he quipped. "Do either of you take milk or sugar? I know you usually take one lump, Evvin."

"That'll be fine." The man smiled and ran a hand through his multicoloured hair.

At least, he continued in his train of thought, this is happening at Phantasies. Any other place might be tense or awkward.

Dhiar had this way of making situations work that would normally not work at all. He effortlessly smoothed over stunted speech and stilted movements with elan, like smoothing out a wrinkled sheet. He drifted this way and that, pouring up the hot water into the cups and then producing a plate of little baked goods from the seemingly endless wellspring that was the cupboard beneath his counter.

"Here you are! They're just cheese biscuits, and I'm afraid they were made yesterday. But still, they ought to be tasty with this tea!"

Evvin looked to Anton and motioned closer to the counter, taking the first steps himself. He walked to the oriel window and pulled the extra chairs over, to sit with Dhiar's larger chair. Anton followed wordlessly behind, curiosity shining in his face.

"I so rarely bother eating," Anton admittedly, slowly lowering himself into one of the seats.

Evvin sat back in his. "Don't say that too loud, Dhiar will fatten you up and you'll love every moment of it!" He finally cracked a grin, resolved with the situation.

The Incubus waved a dismissive hand, all pleased at the praise. He scooped up each cup and saucer in turn, removing the ball and handing the tea over. "Pish-posh! I just whip up little things here and there. I can't imagine not eating food like this... I don't really get the same from it as a human does, for example, but it's still plenty of pleasure to be had."

"Thank you." Anton bowed his head and looked to the cheese

biscuits, reaching out to the plate to pick one up, gingerly, raising it to his mouth.

He hadn't eaten anything at the party. Other than Dhiar, and not much of that, either. Still, if they said it was worthwhile...

"So are we going to start tonight, or are you two too tired from the party?" Evvin raised an eyebrow, an almost wicked expression on his face.

Dhiar turned his head to look at Anton, respectfully deferential. The vampire licked his lips, savoring the bite he had taken, and lost himself in, of the cheese biscuit. So simple, yet so overwhelmingly pleasing.

At last, it dawned on him that all eyes had settled expectantly upon him.

"Oh, er... well... actually..." He cleared his throat, covering his mouth, swallowing the remainder of his mouthful. "Yes, I don't see why not! Why don't we get started?"

"After tea, then!" Dhiar raised his cup in a salute, to both of the others.

9th Night
Funplex

Dhiar's hands moved slowly, gliding across Anton's fine clothing. First he eased his jacket off. Next, the waistcoat, followed by the cravat. The shirt was especially easy, more of an old-style garment, laces rather than buttons. Trousers, socks and garter, and at last the shorts underneath, unassuming but fine, a light white cotton with blue and orange vertical stripes. They were thick enough to be modest, thin enough to make out everything beneath.

Not that it was difficult. The vampire was especially well-endowed. When the shorts came off, it became perfectly clear to Evvin what he had been hiding. His eyebrows raised at the baron's bouncing length. Even if he had been a bit aroused by the Incubus blood's gifts and the sensual strip, it was no less impressive.

"Marvellous, isn't it?" Dhiar reached down to slide his fingers across the steadily-filling length, bringing it to full erection. It nearly reached the man's navel.

If Anton could have blushed, he would have. His eyes closed by themselves, and his breath hitched in his throat. His chest tensed.

"D-Dhiar..."

No matter how many times he found himself in this sort of situation, Evvin always felt self-conscious. "What... are we, er, training to do?"

The young man slowly peeled off his shirt, watching the show before him. He could feel himself getting harder. His hands wandered over his chest, scratching idly here and there, before going to his waist.

"Just sensuality training!" Dhiar tickled his fingertip just under the slit of Anton's cock, between the bulging bulbs of supple skin. "We're going to make Anton into the most sensitive of casanovas. Won't that be fun?"

In less than five seconds, the vampire shot white all over the

floor before him, crying out in a deep voice and collapsing back
against Dhiar. "So... so intense... I can't... it's too..."

"Nonsense!" Dhiar stroked his fingers through the vampire's hair,
easily supporting the taller man's weight. "Evvin, hurry up and
undress. We're going to have a whole night of fun!"

"I can... I can feel him," Anton murmured, opening his eyes and
looking to the lad undressing. His chest rose and fell, breathing rough
as he tried to relax himself. He didn't strictly need to breathe any
longer, but it was one of the few comfortable habits from his life that
he retained.

Dhiar's fingers traced around the light point of Anton's ear. "And
what can you feel about him?"

A silence hung in the room, broken only by the snap of elastic as
Evvin fumbled his waistband. At last he stood, half-erect and naked
in front of the other two. All eyes, he felt, were on him. He never had
considered himself modest or easily humiliated, but it made his
cheeks burn a bit.

"He's embarrassed," Anton replied, at long last.

"Yes," Dhiar continued to speak in soothing tones. "But what
else? Feel it. Feel him. You can tell just by letting yourself go... by
feeling it."

The vampire slowly took a deep breath and closed his eyes, then
let them open again.

"He's excited."

"I think we can see that."

"No, that's not... not like that." Anton fought back a chuckle. "I
mean being naked and being looked at excites him."

Now Dhiar's eyes rested directly on him. Evvin managed a
sheepish grin, averting his gaze to his feet.

A sound almost like a purr came from the Incubus. "Really, now?"

"Really. I can feel it. He likes it." Anton nibbled his lower lip. "I
am... sorry, Evvin. If this was a secret..."

"No, no." Evvin looked back up, stepping around the mess on
the floor to join the two. "I volunteered for this. This is going to be
pretty fun."

Within minutes, Anton's heels were in the air, legs spread, lying draped along the overstuffed chair. Evvin's tongue teased at his entrance, darting out and around. With one hand he pleasured himself.

Dhiar stood nearby, slowly nodding his head, having undressed in that time. "Good, good..." Though erect himself and maintaining it without so much as a caress, he kept himself a few paces away. That would make the other two last longer before reaching climax.

Anton whined, arching his back. His stiff length pulsed and leaped with every touch, every lick... even the ones that Evvin was doing to himself. He could feel it. It was just like Dhiar had warned him it would be. He could feel Evvin stroking himself.

Anton dripped all over his stomach, sticky and slick and clear. He could tell it wouldn't be long. He wanted to linger in the moment forever; it felt so good. His body felt like it would explode. He knew it would only be a matter of time.

A very short time.

He swallowed hard, feeling the tongue intrude. When Dhiar had mentioned it, he never thought it would be anything worth doing. It even seemed a little dirty. A little too naughty. But it felt like heaven...

As the feeling overwhelmed him, his vision went white with sparkles, and he distantly heard himself making the most unbecoming sounds, filling the room with moans and whining. His back arched and his muscles spasmed; he became aware of wetness on his face, in his mouth, salty and rich. He could barely fathom the taste.

Evvin gasped and stumbled back, stunned by the feeling that had hit him like a wall. It was similar to the sensations he enjoyed from Dhiar, but not so elegant. It was just the raw, naked orgasm, with all of the feelings of confusion and disorientation that came with it. Evvin stared ahead blankly as he felt his body respond, spraying the side of the chair and the floor just in front of him with more pearly liquid. He rocked his hips, or rather they rocked themselves, with or without his consent.

"Excellent!" Dhiar clapped his hands, nodding his head with

approval. His smile practically beamed at the two, and he disappeared into the other room.

A short time later he returned; the other two had not yet recovered. But he went to his work with aplomb, not missing a beat. A warm, wet cloth cleaned up each of them, running over their bodies, wiping away the sweat and everything else. Then he cleaned the floor, just like that, and the furniture...

The Incubus had said the place was enormously resistant to stain, but Evvin had never seen it tested. He had a feeling that he would, this night.

10th Night
Mercenary

It was raining again.

It had been raining for some time. At least there was never any hail. But whenever it rained, it covered the whole city like a massive sheet of water. Everything glowed with the bouncing raindrops, white clouds of mist drifting off into nothing with every surface they hit.

"You've never asked."

Dhiar turned his head. He had seated himself in the front window, to watch the rain. Evvin was walking out from behind the silk screen, slowly towards him. To join him.

He climbed into the window, pulling a cushion behind him, reclining opposite Dhiar. The rain steadily drummed all three panes of glass.

"I don't intrude," Dhiar replied. "I feel that if someone has something they wish to tell me, they'll tell me and that will be that."

"Aren't you curious?"

"I would be lying if I said I weren't!" Dhiar let out a little chuckle, turning his head again, to watch the way the drops danced on the street. "But that's for you to choose to tell me. Not for me to choose when you do it. I'll think no less of you, whatever your answer."

Evvin's eyes never once left the Incubus. Silence passed between them.

When at last he spoke, his voice cracked a little. "Are you sure about that?"

Without the slightest hesitation, Dhiar turned to look right into his eyes. That was one of the things that Evvin loved the most about him, and which at times scared him. Whenever Dhiar looked into your eyes, you could feel that he wasn't just looking at your face. He was looking into your soul, past every possible wall or façade you could put up to stop him.

Someone had once said that the eyes were the window to the soul. Evvin could believe it.

"I've never been more certain about anything in my life."

Evvin gathered his knees to his chest and rested his head on them. He hugged his arms around his legs, facing the storm outside.

"I'm just a human."

"There's nothing 'just' about being a human," Dhiar replied, extending a foot to tap lightly at the side of other man's. "It takes tremendous panache to come to a place like this and live, as a human."

"No, I mean..." Evvin hesitated, shoulders falling as he sighed. "I don't want to be just a human. I was... I ran away from home. I wasn't happy there. I didn't like the way the world was, I didn't know where I was going... it was just coincidence that I found the way down here when I did. It was like I found the yellow brick road or something."

The younger man slowly raised his head, sitting back against the wooden wall. He let his legs stretch out, between Dhiar's.

"I didn't know what to do." Evvin flicked his tongue out to wet his lips. His mouth felt dry, his throat tight. "So I just kept walking. When I found this place I thought, well..." he bounced his shoulders, "can't be worse than where I was."

The Incubus reached down to Evvin's sock-foot and took it in his hands, starting to rub it lightly. His touch was not so intense today. Not so edged or full of desire and sex. Evvin felt a relieved sigh escape him.

The Incubus smiled very softly. "Please, relax. No judgement here, not from me."

Evvin let his eyelids drop. He could still hear the rain. He could feel the hands on his foot.

"I didn't really have anyone anymore. Over the years, and all the places, I lost everyone. Or they went away. Or everything seemed to stand between us. And even though we went everywhere, there was nowhere that filled that... hole. In me." He opened his eyes, lashes wet with little drops of moisture. His voice shook quietly.

"Well, I know all about filling holes! You've come to the right place." Dhiar's expression remained warm, tone as irreverent as always.

Evvin opened his mouth, at first surprised and confused... and then he laughed, a deep, heartfelt laugh of relief. Tears poured down his cheeks, and he rocked forward, right into Dhiar's arms, into the embrace that pulled him to the Incubus's chest.

After the brief laughter faded, it was replaced with sobs, wracking his body, wetting the demon's shirt. The rain roared louder outside, and it seemed only to taper off when the tears did. Evvin sniffed, pushing his palms at his cheeks, to wipe the wetness away.

"It's all right," Dhiar whispered to him, tilting his chin up. "You're not alone, and you'll never be alone again if you don't want to be. You've got forever to decide what you want to be. How to fill that gap. There's a whole world out there, and a whole universe too. I won't rest until you can be happy with your existence."

Evvin impulsively leaned up, to touch his lips to Dhiar's. It was just a short little kiss. But at that moment, it meant so much to him. It was everything. The world was in that kiss.

Dhiar squeezed his arms around Evvin, rocking slowly from side to side. "You don't have to worry. You don't have to feel pushed. We have all the time in the world. I won't force anything on you. Except I will make sure you eat well." He flashed a grin, matched by the man in his arms. "If you don't want to be a human, well... there are all kinds of other things you can be. Even being a human, you can be all kinds of other things. There are people who ride in human shells but are just waiting to emerge from that cocoon."

Evvin placed his head on Dhiar's shoulder. The rain was getting stronger again. "Sorry for... you know. Being emotional. I just feel so lost sometimes. Everyone else here seems to know what they want, you know? It feels hard to keep up when you don't have wings or fangs or an amazing aura." He smiled a little bit. "Or gourmet chef ability."

"You should never apologise for having emotions." Dhiar stroked a hand through the man's hair. "Anyone who expects that is a person who is dishonest with themselves. Or a rock. And if it's a rock, why are you apologising to it for having emotions?" He patted Evvin's head, resting his hand there. "Just do your thing. Live the way you want to. Plenty of the people here were thrust into their lives without any choice on their part. Some of the vampires, for example... you might think they've got it all together, but plenty of them were made into what they are by accident, or without thinking about all of the repercussions. But most of them do their own thing, their way."

"I guess I never thought of it that way." Evvin took a deep breath, sitting up. "Thank you."

"Thank you," Dhiar answered, cupping his cheek. "I'm honored by you telling me these things. That you trust me enough."

"I think I trust you more than I've ever trusted anyone. Ever."

Dhiar wove his fingers with Evvin's, squeezing with affection.

11th Night
Help, I'm Alive

This part of the city wasn't really a proper part of the city. It had been, once, but with the migration—a slow migration, given the general longevity of its inhabitants—it was simply left to deteriorate, to become as dilapidated and abandoned as it had. It was easy to see that the place had once been grand and beautiful. It still possessed a certain beauty, but one tinged with sadness; nothing new had been built in ages.

The primary reasoning behind this was that it had become a kind of relic itself, and home to relics. The oldest vampire of the city, the most ancient demon, could not compare to the age of the youngest revenant. Even if physically they remained young, there was something about them... something about their dark eyes, their pallid, cool bodies... the way they moved, the unnatural silence with which they seemed to do everything.

And here Dhiar found himself, in the midst of the buildings overgrown with moss and vine, masonry cracked and split, wood of construction mixed with the slender woody tendrils of the plants that thrived in the underground.

"Love the decor," the Incubus commented, crossing one leg atop the other and sitting back in a chair that was probably once especially fine. "It's got such distinctiveness to it!"

"I'm grateful for you coming to deliver to me." The man to whom he spoke was one of the very same revenants who made up the majority of the district's population.

His hair framed his face, styled haphazardly, a red so dark as to appear almost black in the low light. It matched his eyes. His skin, of course, was palest white. Bone white. And the clothes covering his body were aged, to say the least: fine cloth and tapestry, but frayed and worn, though not yet threadbare.

Dhiar wiggled his fingers. "Money's money! Anyway, I thought

I might be able to bring a little cheer to a place that was supposed to be fairly dismal. Really, though, I think it has a charm of its own." He glanced around the room again. "It's at least honest. No pretence. No façades. It is what it is. In a half-reclaimed-by-nature way."

"This place is the past and the future of Noctemburg," the revenant replied, walking to the crate brought from Phantasies. "Every part has come from this, every part will go to this, when they grow tired of it. The Earth has its own ways of addressing things. Oh, this is perfect. Perfect!"

Dhiar loved a challenge. Like vampires, revenants tended to be on the cooler side of body temperature. Unlike vampires, however, revenants rarely indulged in the sensual pleasures, rarely enjoyed each other's company. They merely went about their undead existences in a sort of silent commiseration.

They did not speak of the zombies. Those were unfortunates, barely ambulatory, barely even undead...

So different from the man in Dhiar's eyes, into whose tone some happiness had seeped. It made his eyes light up. He looked almost lively.

"I don't believe I caught your name," Dhiar at last spoke, pushing himself to his feet and walking over to his customer.

"Lothring," he answered, turning to face the Incubus, holding the tunic up along his chest proudly. "Does it suit me?"

"Very much." Dhiar reached his hands out and began to unfasten the buttons of the man's waistcoat, so easily, so casually. "Let's try it on."

"What... what are you doing?" If Lothring could have blushed, he would have. "I..."

"I'm helping you to undress. It's a luxury that few have, you know." Dhiar glanced up, into the darkest eyes he had ever seen. "It's imperative I make my customer happy."

The touch alone sent bolts of ecstasy through Lothring. He felt himself overwhelmed, and his fingers fumbled at the tunic. The battle was lost, and the garment tumbled back to the crate, draping over its side. He didn't always remember to breathe, but it seemed

right this time. He felt his breath catch in his throat. A soft sound came from his chest.

Dhiar slowly worked the waistcoat down the man's arms and off them, then began to undo the buttons of his shirt. "I haven't seen a shirt of this style in at least twenty years. It's beautiful. I wish it would come back in style again. It makes a man look... delicious."

Lothring, however, could not manage to form words. Had it really been that long? This was the newest clothing of his wardrobe! Had it really been that long... since...

"Your skin... is luscious." Dhiar leaned in to kiss at the centre of the revenant's chest, the skin there cool but not cold. Just like the demeanor of the man: aloof, but not unreachable, and warming by the second.

The Incubus slowly opened the shirt, working it down the shoulders, over the man's arms, leaving it at the forearms to fix the arms back. He took in the lean musculature, the erect nipples, the barely-visible sigils tinting the skin from distant rituals that had faded. Delicately he applied his tongue to the right nipple, tracing the tip around the areola, then dipping to the nub, teasing it.

The bare skin touching, the attention, all of it washed over Lothring like a wave crashing on his unready shore. His mouth hung open, his eyes glazed with stunned indulgence. His trousers were so tight. Somehow his clothes must have shrunk.

No, he thought, that's not how it goes. That's not what this is.

What was forgotten for a moment came flooding back, when Dhiar's wandering hands found his trousers and worked them slowly down. Somehow it had become cooler and warmer at the same time. He could not remember the last time he noticed the temperature, or that it affected him at all.

As he felt another lick, this time at his left nipple, he trembled. Moving his arms to let the shirt drop to the floor, he lifted his hand and ran it through the Incubus's magnificent curls.

Oh help, the words flicked through his mind. It's so beautiful. So wonderful. I'm drowning in it.

He let himself go under.

12th Night
Black Sheep

"More! *More!*" Dhiar felt Lothring inside him, deep inside. And this time, it was so hot, churning inside as it filled him. He hummed little moans of pleasure, slowly licking his lips.

The other man panted, though he did not strictly need to breathe. He grinned wickedly down at the Incubus, chest rising and falling. His eyes smouldered, fire dancing within their ruby depths. He liked that Dhiar's eyes were almost the same colour as his own.

"Ohh... more..." Dhiar reached up to run a hand along Lothring's side, laughing deep, a rumbling vibrating in his throat. "More..."

"Mein lieber Dhiar," Lothring quipped, tensing his muscles and then easing into the touch, "we have already had no less than five rolls in the proverbial hay. Surely you cannot want more."

But he only teased, and he reached his hand to trace his fingertips over the top of the demon's. It was so much warmer than his own. He found that heat addictive.

"More, then." Lothring reached down to pull Dhiar atop him as he rolled onto his back. "But we switch off again! Now you, you give me more."

The Incubus leaned up to lock lips, massaging, suckling, nipping, as his hands wandered all over the other man's body. So hot... such heat mingled between them. Without words, Dhiar began to grind his crotch against Lothring's, already rigid and supple, dripping with slickness, body fragrant with the sweat of arousal.

Some revenants took little regard of their bodies, but Lothring always kept his well-fed and well-tended. He healed any injury, maintained the energies he could, and though he did not tax it unnecessarily, he also did not sit sedentary like some of them. He could not imagine continuing to exist as a barely-ambulatory bag of bones in flesh, custodian to some ruined architecture long past its prime or a library blanketed in dust.

And at this moment, he felt more lively than he had in ages. Decades, surely. Dhiar did not ease into him; he didn't need to, after all of their fun in the day up to that point. By now, the two had become comfortably relaxed with each other, just enough to make things easier.

He could feel the warmth dribbling onto his body from within Dhiar, the warmth that he had put there. They had exchanged fluids so many times that they almost seemed like the same being. He shivered and became even more aroused, tensing his stomach and clenching his buttocks, tightening his passage around Dhiar's perfectly-sized, perfectly-shaped length.

Meanwhile, the Incubus gazed down into Lothring's eyes. Even if the rest of him enchanted so, enthralled him so, the eyes always caught him. This could be an ideal partner, Dhiar mused. Revenants don't really get tired, can go at a moment's notice, and are never in any danger of going without food or drink.

At the same time, similar thoughts flicked through Lothring's mind. He could barely feel the bed beneath him. It seemed more like clouds.

And the benevolent Moon smiling down upon him was Dhiar, rose-kissed skin and hematite hair... boundless reserves of energy to share between them... he could get pieces from other foods, but there was nothing quite like the primal essence of living. The Incubus exuded it like a heat lamp.

Another kiss began, the thrusting slapping him like a spanking. His balls quaked and bounced, sac loose and soft, draping over his body. His cock sprayed drops of precum like little drops of syrup all over his stomach, and he shivered. So much had come back to him. He felt so much attachment, now, to living rather than existing. Even if technically unlife, he saw so much now, so much that he had heretofore neglected.

"More... more!" Lothring would have blushed if his body

allowed it. He found himself muffled, thankfully. His feelings mirrored the words of the Incubus only a few moments earlier.

At least the bed was more luxurious than the first three rounds, which had been on the carpet. Dhiar's enticing way of undressing the revenant led to quick, dirty fucking. Naturally, neither of them minded.

"My stars," Lothring murmured, arching his back sharply as Dhiar slipped down from his lips, to bite little nibbles down his neck. "Don't stop. Don't stop."

When the Incubus began to lap along the side, with the tongue of his, rougher than a human's, that was enough. Lothring erupted high enough to hit Dhiar's cheek and covered his stomach. He could not stop whimpering, utterly consumed by the pleasure. It soon hit Dhiar, and he filled the other man, slowing his rhythm and lying atop him.

"Well," he broke the silence, after a few minutes of catching breath. "You certainly seem to be enjoying yourself."

Lothring turned, lips parting, expression a mixture of curiosity and surprise. He paused, rather than speaking immediately, and flicked his tongue over his lips. His eyes thoughtfully regarded the Incubus.

"I intend to have you become a regular delivery boy. Will that be acceptable?"

"Fine by me! But..." Dhiar tapped the tip of Lothring's nose, "I will insist upon payment being tendered in similar fashion. I must have standards, you know."

The revenant laughed, shaking the both of them with the quaking of his chest. He slid his arms around Dhiar and squeezed with affection, pulling him up like a blanket, regardless of the state of each of their bodies.

"I wouldn't dream of contradicting a business agreement. But don't let me pull you away from other... customers."

"I wouldn't dream of shafting a client," Dhiar replied, then he paused. "So to speak."

The two of them began to laugh at once, the laughter melting into kisses, the kisses slowly igniting into bodies moving against each other.

The evening had only just begun. An afternoon's play could so easily turn into a night's amusement. Little else presented itself in this district of antiquity and silence. The heat began to rise again, and for an instant, even in this place, for just a little while... it felt like summer.

13th Night
Twilight Galaxy

"Evvin, darling!"

The Incubus's voice rang through the shop's sales floor. Soon, the well-pierced and increasingly well-groomed man appeared before him, smiling and waving. His eyes held a sheepish spark in them.

Dhiar threw his arms around Evvin, pulling him close and pressing a kiss to his lips. Just for a moment, he lingered; just a little longer than necessary.

"How's business been?" He ran his fingertip along Evvin's ear, around the bumps and curves of his many rings and studs. "Sorry to have stayed away so long. I intended to just go and come back, but well... you know how one thing leads to another. Got a regular order out of it."

Evvin slid his arms along Dhiar's shoulders, leaning in for another sweet kiss, then another. "Anton came by, so I... did my best to help him keep himself fresh. Just in case you sprang a pop quiz on him."

"Oh, did you now..."

"We, er, ended up just going over some things we'd covered before."

"Brought up a few things between you."

"Exactly." Evvin's cheeks pinkened just a touch.

"Well, darling," Dhiar answered, moving his hand down to swat the other man's backside, "it's dinnertime and I've missed you terribly. What would you like to eat tonight? And..."

"And...?"

"And what would you like to do, afterwards?"

The gleam in Evvin's eyes told the Incubus everything he needed to know.

Each person's body was different, even in subtle ways. The

discrepancies between the revenant and this vital, vibrant young man were endless. Both of them were an endless pleasure. Dhiar's mind swam in ecstasy as he felt another orgasm wash over him and splash along Evvin's psyche.

"That's... that'll never be anything but amazing," Evvin sighed, arching his back.

Dhiar slid smoothly out and dropped atop the man, rubbing cheek to cheek. "For me too."

"That's something that always kind of made me wonder." Evvin stretched his arms up and tucked one behind his head, the other snaking around Dhiar's chest. "I would've thought you'd get tired of it, after this long. I can't believe it doesn't get old."

"You said yourself it would never be anything but amazing, for you..." The Incubus turned his head, kissing down Evvin's cheek to the corner of his mouth. "It's the same with me. When it's someone new, it's like an undiscovered land, all fresh and secret and hidden, for me to uncover. When it's a lover I know, it's a comfortable terrain that will never cease to surprise and arouse me. And amaze me."

The wind whistled outside the window. Heavy rains buffeted the glass almost instantly. It sounded like small pebbles thrown up against the side of the building.

"Always the perfect thing to say," Evvin murmured, tilting his mouth up to catch Dhiar's. "I wonder if it'll rain all night."

"All night," Dhiar replied, "and through tomorrow. Maybe the next day too."

"Ah! Amongst all your other talents, you're a meteorologist?"

The Incubus slid his body to the side, dragging his still-full length along the other man's hip, to just below his navel. "No, but the fellow I was delivering to has many talents. Among them is a curious but rather adorable interest in the weather movements of this place. He's got... he's got this grand place, it's like a celestial dome or something, and he's... it's modelled after the city. But it's more than the city. It's this whole model of all of it, and it's amazing..."

"Sometimes I miss the stars." Evvin reached up, a gasp hitching in his throat as he felt Dhiar's most intimate parts across his stomach again. "Sometimes the painted ones aren't enough for me."

Dhiar's eyes at once seemed like inscrutable pools of garnet and fluffy little pansy-petals. His brows curved, his mouth lowered again to kiss Evvin's, and he slowly breathed in.

"One day, you'll find your stars."

Barely a whisper. Barely enough to be heard, scarcely the sound of an utterance. Yet it lingered in the air. It rang bell-clear, cut through the din on the outside walls that filled the air.

"What do you mean?" Evvin started his hand moving again, fingertips brushing along the middle of his lover's back. "Did he tell you something about me, too?"

"It's nothing I haven't known from the moment I first met you." Dhiar brushed his lips on the tip of Evvin's nose. "I've always seen the stars in your eyes. But you want stars outside them too. That's always how it goes. When you're a star, you can't gaze upon yourself. That isn't how it works."

No words passed between them for a time, the only sound in the place coming from the downpour hitting wood and brick and glass.

The soft lamps glowed, flickering from time to time as power and energy fluctuated with natural rush and tumult. The whistling of the breeze drowned with the water showering down around it.

"I'll just admit it," Evvin answered. "I don't quite get what you just said, but I think it makes some sense to me." He began to grin. "But you're... well, you're not like a star, I can't say that. You're more like a Moon or a Sun or something..."

"Some kind of heavenly body," Dhiar teased.

"Something like that."

"You need stars to make your lovely little romantic twilight galaxy," Dhiar whispered, his breath tickling Evvin's skin. "Anton's a bright lovely star, burning bright like a tyger. And you've been touched by the light of other things... shooting stars, comets, meteorites... but that's all part of the journey, you know."

The young man let breath fill his chest, eyelids falling closed. "You think... do you think we could... take a trip? Leave here? Ever?"

Dhiar moved his body down, lowering his head to rest on Evvin's chest, closing his own eyes. "It's not my time to leave here." He uncurled his fingers and rubbed his palm along his lover's shoulder. "But Anton's got a chateau, and if he's asked you away, you really should take the opportunity. Life's one of those things that, even if you have forever, sometimes these chances only present themselves once in a very long time."

"If I do," Evvin continued, "when I come back... will you be here? Will I... I'll see you again, won't I?"

"Even if I'm not here, I promise you... we will see each other again, if you wish it." Dhiar raised his head and leaned down to kiss Evvin's mouth.

This time, it was as if they mingled in existence. It was like becoming the same person again, two figures that had separated, for whatever reason, early in life and only now had reunited. Hearts beat as one, breath came in and escaped again.

"Oh Dhiar." Evvin squeezed his arms around the Incubus. "I love you so much. It's crazy. I love you so much."

14th Night
Jidai (Time Goes Around)

Dhiar could not face the warm colours of the neon in the front window of Phantasies. It just burned at his eyes. The lonely shop only reminded him how much he missed Evvin already.

But he had to do what was right. And there was always the happiness of having had what they had. It wasn't over, not as such... but he knew how things like this tended to go. At least he also knew that the young man would be happy.

The Incubus rarely came to the fancier parts of town. It wasn't that the prices were outside of his range; eternity made the accumulation of money a simple matter. The people there, however, tended to make him feel like an outsider. The part of town with Phantasies and the nearby club, even if a little dirty and unprestigious, possessed a certain homely trait to it. It felt like home, much moreso than the rest of the city.

He pushed open the door to a bookshop. Inside, it glowed as if all afire, the warm, soft lights given new depth by all the wooden shelves, the walls panelled with cherry wood, and the countless books, one after the other packed together. Side by side they stood. He could not estimate how old most of them must have been. But despite their apparent age, the place had scarcely a speck of dust on its shelves.

Dhiar took in a breath through his nose. The scent of old paper mixed with the citrus aroma of clean wood. His boots clicked against sleek wood, until they reached the narrow carpets lining the aisles.

Books were always something he could rely upon. Even if he couldn't make time to sweep back to Dis, back to his birthplace, he could at least travel in his mind to other destinations. He reached up to tug one of the tomes off the shelf and laid it open between his palms.

Barely a handful of words flashed before his eyes, and then a sweet voice met his ears.

"I don't think I've seen you here before. Welcome."

He turned to settle his eyes onto the woman who spoke: dark golden hair, inky eyes, and a fashion flair for reds, golds, and browns, an ideal match to the decor of the shop.

"Oh!" Dhiar closed the book and turned to replace it on the shelf. "Thank you! I've just been a bit restless, I thought I might visit the city I so rarely see."

"I don't get out much either." She laughed and extended her hand, though in a delicate way, a way of a lady not entirely accustomed to the modern age. "I am Miranda."

"Dhiar." He dipped down to kiss her hand, bringing it up to his lips, and released it as he rose again.

A look of surprised satisfaction crossed her face. Her lips stretched into a smile. "It's been a quiet time, lately. I haven't had a visitor in three days. Would you like... if you do not think it forward, that is... would you like to share a glass of wine? We could discuss books. Perhaps I could help you to find a story that would please you."

"Naturally, I'd love to."

"Excellent." She swept her hand to the centre of the shop, farther inside.

It had many qualities like Phantasies: it was so warm, so welcoming, and full of things arranged in a way that made it seem larger than it actually was. The colours all soothed the eye, like a wonderful fluffy blanket in midwinter. He felt comforted just by being there.

They continued to a sort of love sofa, made of rich red-tinted wood and scarlet cushions of velveteen. Dhiar lowered himself to one end, watching as his hostess slipped off into the maze of bookshelves and rectangular wooden pillars, the flattering fabric of her dress rippling behind her.

Maybe he just needed another place as comforting as Phantasies, but in a different way. This bookshop seemed to be a kindred spirit. He let a sigh pass from his lips and, for a moment, let his eyes close.

"I hope you like red," Miranda's voice came from nearby, and Dhiar's eyes instantly opened again. "My favourite is Spanish wine."

Dhiar sat up a little straighter. "The company is what makes a wine great. I'm sure it will be a pleasure for both of us."

Her cheeks coloured as she sat, handing the bottle to Dhiar and setting two glasses down on the table before the sofa. She motioned to him and produced a corkscrew.

In his hands he took it, and screwed it in the cork, working it out easily and smoothly. Handing the cork to her, he poured up two splashes of the wine in the glasses. "There. Let's have a taste of the aroma first."

She ran the cork just under her lips, parting them and breathing in. Her lips curled upward, and she reached over to accept her glass from him, bringing it up to her face. This aroma, this tickled her palette. She took the slightest of sips and held it on her tongue. In seconds, it unfolded to spice, and sweetness, and slid down her throat.

"Yes, it's wonderful, isn't it?" Miranda returned the glass to the table.

Dhiar slowly nodded his head. "Marvellous."

As if automatically, he picked up the bottle and filled their glasses this time, setting it down again and holding out Miranda's glass to her. Then he took his own and raised it.

"To absent friends."

She lifted her own glass, the ruby liquid inside shimmering as the lights danced in it. It seemed, in that moment, like a mask for her and a well for Dhiar's thoughts and emotions. They swirled in its depths, in the infinite depths of a single glass, tinted the slightest of greens. It made it look older.

Miranda, however, looked ever younger, more innocent, perhaps more vulnerable. He had not met a woman like her for many, many years. It had defied his expectation so much. But perhaps that was what he needed, on this solitary night.

She inclined her head slightly forward. "To absent friends."

15th Night
Slow Surfing

Dhiar pulled the laces at his hips free and worked his trousers down in the front. The cool air felt so good against his skin, especially between his legs. That always seemed to get hotter than anywhere else.

A little shiver ran along the small of his back as he began to relieve himself in the garden. Watering the trees, as he had put it. It was nice that Lothring actually managed to maintain some semblance of order in what had become a strange garden of chaos. This antiquated part of the city, moved past and largely forgotten, was overgrown and overrun. Except the revenant's garden and his old house.

It wasn't in the best of repair, by any means. But then he didn't need it to be.

Dhiar shook off and tucked himself back in, pulling his trousers back up around his waist and lacing them... but loosely. He returned to the conservatory overlooking the garden. "Thanks!"

"Really, there's no trouble. You could have used the chamberpot." Lothring sat stock-still in his wingback chair of cream the same colour as aged bones. "I find it quite convenient."

The Incubus waved a hand, walking over to the chair. "Somehow, there's a loss of mystery when one uses the chamberpot, I find... just the sound of it all, you know..." And without pausing a moment, he lowered himself to drape across Lothring's lap. "I'm so glad to be here, and I'm delighted you seem to be enjoying the things I bring you."

"Well," Lothring answered, reaching down to pull the laces apart, pulling the front of the dark, tender material away from the reddish skin, "I enjoy one thing more than all of the other things, of course. But I suppose you knew that."

"I knew that." Dhiar gave a toothy, bright, wide grin, eyes sparkling as they did when he knew it was going to go somewhere naughty.

Lothring's cool hand slid down the treasure trail from navel to the fluffy black mass shimmering over Dhiar's crotch. The Incubus leaned heavily against the other man's chest, spreading his legs, sending one angled down at the floor as the other curled along the arm of the chair.

The revenant slid his fingers from the base to the head, taking the length in his hand and pulling it up. A little leftover drop of moisture sparkled at the tip, like a tiny jewel. It vanished from sight as Dhiar began to stiffen and rise.

The Incubus breathed out and then sharply in again, letting his consciousness wander. His skin pricked up, so sensitive, and a different sort of moisture formed a little jewel-droplet along the slit at the very tip of his penis. Lothring, without saying a word, pressed it with his first finger and traced circles, spirals in and out, eventually covering the entire head with slickness as it presented itself.

The revenant's fingers danced along inner thigh, from one to the other, and over the velvet pouch dangling between. Its contents were so heavy, yet they bounced at the touch as if some small pulley inside had jerked one's side, then the other. It amused Lothring.

He left the erection alone and slid down, down the underside of it, down over the balls again and then under them... tracing the little line between the legs, until he found the bud of raised muscle. And there he barely caressed, barely a slickened fingertip to trace its oblong shape. His lips curled up, and he drew the tip of his tongue over the front of his teeth.

Dhiar dripped like a faucet in anticipation. He had been saving up for this; whenever he visited Lothring, he never really knew when it would happen, or even if it would happen, but this time he needed it. He depended on it. Revenants were always so hard to read. He felt the warm drip-drop just below his navel. His breathing became quicker and more shallow.

He wanted to cry out, to tell him he could have everything, but the only sound that his vocal chords managed to produce was a long, low moan. He closed his eyes and let his head drop against Lothring's shoulder. His shoulders and chest rose and fell as one, his excitement uncontrollable.

At last, the revenant's nimble fingers curled around Dhiar's length again and began to stroke it. The Incubus could not help himself; he lifted his hips in need. His lips parted, and he almost panted at the intense sensation washing over him. His aura shared it with Lothring. He knew it was being felt by both of them. But that was another thing about revenants: they could be so stoic, one would never know it until they released in the palm of one's hand.

But he could tell Lothring only played with stoicism, now. He let himself be ebullient around Dhiar, around his weekly delivery. The shopkeeper had awakened something in him, something that had slept for far too long, something unique to this outmoded district.

It was a newness that made it all the more special. The first time on delivery day was always the most unexpected. When would it happen? What would it come from? Where would it go to? These questions always flashed through Dhiar's head as he sat on the metro, then rode the carriage.

He absently wondered if the horses were revenants too. They always seemed unnaturally quiet.

But all thought of anything other than Lothring was quickly pushed from his mind. He opened his eyes and gazed at him, and the man gazed back, grinning that wicked grin. The most vital, playful, wicked, wonderful grin.

Dhiar gasped, forgetting himself and then remembering. His muscles tensed, his voice caught in his throat, and he nearly choked. Lothring slid the Incubus's shirt up suddenly, all the way to his armpits, and less than five seconds later, Dhiar felt himself shooting warm and sticky over his stomach.

He released a sound, a sound like a sustained note, and it slowly rose and fell again. His breath left him in a slow sigh. He closed his eyes and curled against Lothring.

"Again?"

16th Night
Never Be Mine

Dhiar enjoyed parties, but all things considered, he was more of a homebody. Some Incubi and Succubi were social butterflies, always loving the party of the moment; Chana was like that. His sister thrived on parties, on mingling, and could make a rather fine existence off canapés and whatever champagne the host fancied. He could see her, in his mind, with best friend and lover Lilly, smoking cigarettes in those long holders with the flower design at the end.

How they loved that! Dhiar wondered if that was the kind of life he would end up getting used to, in time. He would have to ring her up sometime soon. Maybe that was a better idea than watching Noctemburg slowly roll to a halt.

It did seem like a train, in that. He knew it would only be a relatively short time before its wheels began to run again and the sound of thick smoke chuffing through the stack filled the air. It would once again be loud and busy and people everywhere.

Just like this party. The Incubus was actually surprised at how loud and busy it was, and how many people were in attendance. Perhaps, he thought, they had hoped to get the wheels turning again.

These were people who didn't normally socialise. Some of them, anyway. Whoever the host of this party was, he or she had managed to work a few minor miracles to assemble the group. At least he remained in one of the more neutral categories. And not another Incubus in sight! So he figured, at least, he and the vampires would likely have their pick of partners for later.

"Let me guess," a voice rang from behind Dhiar, "you're looking around to pick out someone for a tumble."

The Incubus turned, and his eyes settled onto a vision that made him catch his breath: tall, well-built, mid-length hair that went from black to a sort of pinkish white. Broad-necked blouse, a couple of bracelets, and if those trousers were any tighter, they'd be behind him. Behind him with his iridescent feathery wings, with golden tinges at the top.

"I..." For the first time in a long time, Dhiar fumbled with his words. Oh, how he wanted that! But there were considerations. Especially at a party of this type. "Actually," he managed, "I was looking for the punch bowl. I haven't had punch in ages, and I heard it was really tasty tonight."

A slightly thick brow raised on the other man, and he raised his hand, uncurled a finger, and pointed in the direction of the refreshments. They took up a whole side of the room.

Not even missing a beat, Dhiar held out his hand in invitation. "Want to get some punch with me? I could use some pleasant company."

"I'm surprised you haven't already got plenty of that. Where are you hiding them?" The winged man slowly broke into a tentative grin. "I'm called Siros."

"Dhiar!" The Incubus reached out and took the other man's hand, weaving his fingers and smiling as he pulled him along to the punch bowl.

There was a certain consideration: he looked awfully like the stereotypical angel, and those types tended to be rather exclusive. They were always nice to look at—usually rather nice in bed too—but a whole load of issues he didn't want to open up. Most of the ones in Noctemburg were "free angels", which was to say they were currently unattached as messengers; no deity impressing things upon them, no real restrictions... but some of them still lived by the codes that they used to, and so often that led to friction.

That was to say nothing of the actual *attached* ones, who simply lived in the city out of preference.

"So do you always opt for punch when there's wine, or is this just an exception?" Siros stood by as the two cups were filled.

"Just a craving! I'm a little picky with wines, but my sister can put anything away, I think. Drinks me under the table." Dhiar passed the man one of the ornate frosted-glass cups, taking the other for himself and lifting it. "To wings!"

"To horns," Siros answered, grinning broader and touching his cup to Dhiar's, before he tipped it to his own lips. "Mm. That is very good punch. They must have used fresh fruit."

"Undoubtedly! And speaking of which, I've been wondering if you'd like to take a walk in the gardens. I hear they're exquisite."

At first, Siros's face showed some slight confusion. Then he supposed that, in fact, the gardens were the origin of the fruit. That made sense, as a segue. So he finished his little cup and set it back down, on the tray of the used cups, to be cleaned and returned. Dhiar did the same, keeping his hand in the angelic man's.

They passed through the crowds largely disregarded; there were too many other interesting people around who were actively trying to engage others, instead of trying to get away from them. Soon, the two were surrounded in comparative quiet. The party seemed miles away, with the lushness of the gardens.

"Really stunning." Absently, Dhiar leaned a bit against Siros and wondered what the gardens must look like during the day. He caught himself doing that so often, even though he had lived in Noctemburg for years now. "I love moonflowers."

"Me too." Siros's voice had such depth to it, such sweetness on the edges, but the substance of it was a little rough, and quite deep. "You have to, to live here."

Dhiar turned his head slightly. "I meant to ask, by the way... I hope you don't mind me taking your hand..."

"Eh? No, of course not!" Siros started to laugh, spreading his wings out and curling one around Dhiar, the other around his own side. "I used to serve a love-god, actually..."

"Oh... oh really?" Dhiar squeezed the angel's hand.

"Mm. I just needed some time to my own... and I had served him well, so he provided for me to come here for a time..."

The Incubus started grinning uncontrollably. They were surrounded by night-scented stock. It mixed in his mind with affection and turned the world upside-down. It was all upside-down. The chill of the endless night made the other man's presence even warmer. His wings were so soft, so very soft and delightful. He wanted to pull them around him like a blanket...

17th Night
Under the Ivy

Dhiar swore he could see fireworks as his eyes opened again. He inhaled rose-scented air, the blooms all around him. The white roses were open, smiling out at the world, and his lips were on Siros's, so soft and pink and delicate.

The angel looked so much like a marble statue, a magnificently enthralling combination of delicate and masculine. Dhiar could feel his body, so close, a mixture too: at the same time soft and accommodating, and sturdy and muscular. He couldn't resist, couldn't stop himself, and he found himself embracing Siros, arms curled tightly about his chest.

He could feel the warmth of his heart... or was that hearts? No-one was ever sure with him, and he was never entirely sure with anyone else in the city. He supposed it didn't actually matter.

They wandered about the place, kissing, touching, feeling each other. Their bodies touched, crashing waves upon each other's shore, and then drew back. It was the undercurrent that pulled, the powerful vortex drawing them deeper.

Dhiar had almost become drunk on Siros, and his own scent mingled with lady of the night. The slender little blossoms beckoned from halfway across the garden. He had grown to love them. It made the whole thing seem more like a lovely, beautiful dream. So many marvellous flowers, thriving in this deep shade. The path was marked by primrose. How appropriate, he thought.

But they veered off the path and found themselves lying tangled in each other, under a wall covered in ivy. It may have even been made entirely of ivy; it was impossible to tell anything else that made it up. Dhiar marvelled at the feelings washing over his body.

"You weren't kidding when you said you worked for a love-god," he murmured, reaching out to run his fingers along the delicately-curled ends of Siros's locks.

"No, it was... rewarding. Often, anyway."

"Often?"

"Love is simple and kind. And cruel, at times. It always conquers, it always prevails... but sometimes it doesn't do that in the happiest ways. There are many kinds of love... and sometimes, even when you'd like one kind of love, you get another. So close, and so far away, all at the same time..."

The words hit him, and Dhiar leaned in for another kiss. He preferred them this way, really. He liked the sweet kisses, just the lips. There was so much to do with lips, massaging and pulling, suckling and nibbling... a cornucopia of possibilities. He caught his breath again.

"Sorry," Siros pulled back, licking his lips. "Maybe I'm forcing this. I've been lonely, I'm sorry. This isn't fair to you..."

Dhiar's lips remained apart. "Eh? No, no. I mean, you're the most beautiful man here, why shouldn't I enjoy your company?"

"Appearances aren't everything."

"I'm not talking," Dhiar purred, "about how you look on the outside." He ran his fingertips down the side of the man's neck. "Although that's lovely too. Beautiful... well, it's different than pretty, it's different because you have a certain quality that comes through in your voice and the way you carry yourself. I can tell you're kind and loving. If you were just pretty but arrogant, or pretty and cruel, like plenty of the angels living in this place, well... I wouldn't have anything to do with you. Wouldn't give you time of day."

Dhiar chuckled as Siros raised an eyebrow. The Incubus moved his hand along the loose material of the perfect white blouse, feeling the pectoral curve beneath his palm. "So to speak."

The Incubus swore he could hear thunder. He took a deep breath and lifted a leg, rubbing the inside of his knee along the outside of Siros's hip. Leaning in, he gave another sweet kiss, then another... the angel's lips tasted so sweet. So soft, they beckoned like a pillow for his head.

"Is it going to storm?" Siros spoke up, tone unconcerned.

"Probably."

The lightning was new. The thunder was new. Originally, Noctemburg had neither, just condensation collecting and centuries of magic rolling into cloud cover. Lately, however, with the rains had come the actual storm. It was the part Dhiar loved the most. Thunder always felt so right. It moved his body, down to the core of it, down to the root. He could feel it, vibrating him, shaking everything, virile and manly and beautiful.

It made the soft surface of the garden feel even more intoxicatingly like drifting on air. He couldn't tell whether it was grasses or mosses; few lights illuminated their walk. The luminous mushrooms only just marked the way to walk.

"Would you like to come to my place?" Siros let his fingers wander over Dhiar's cheek. "Unless of course you'd like to stay at the party and organise an orgy. I'm sure you'd be very good at that..."

"I'll leave that to my sister and her parties." Dhiar touched the tip of his nose against Siros's, then captured his mouth again, for only an instant. "Is it far? We might want to wait out the rain..."

Before he could finish, the sheets of water fell. Suddenly, everything went to the wayside, and Dhiar found himself on his back, the full weight of Siros atop him. It wasn't more than he could handle. Those wings practically covered the both of them.

The angel was shielding him from the rain. He smiled from above. Dhiar almost wept, so touched by the gesture. He leaned up and kissed him, good and hard. The Incubus let the very tips of his fingernails trace through the fabric of the angel's shirt, over his chest, over his aroused nipples, down his sides, over his navel...

"I guess this means I won't be able to fly you there," Siros murmured, out of breath. He leaned down and returned the kiss anyway, barely teasing with his tongue, lips parted just so.

Dhiar kept losing himself in the kisses. The very part that was Dhiar, the very thing that made up his essence, now seemed adrift in a sea of storms and angels. He could scarcely centre himself. He didn't want to centre himself.

"I think we've already flown," he whispered.

18th Night
The Other Side of Life

It wasn't at all what Dhiar had expected, this place. It was almost like an experiment in décor and architecture, but fully appealing: everything seemed warm and inviting, no real walls, and only a few windows, easily hidden by drapes. Those drapes, as well as tapestries and cloth hangings, made the borders of the room. It looked a bit like what a harem might resemble, in some elaborate fantasy.

It reminded Dhiar of home. The lazy, luxurious lounges full of cushions, made into dreamlike mazes of diaphanous fabrics that shone like they were made of sugar; he couldn't help himself and remembered the Pit, the most fabulous club in Dis. All around its massive aquatic column were bars, seats, and of course those same lounges.

He felt like asking if Siros had ever been to the Great City, but he couldn't decide if that might be rude or not, so he swallowed it.

"I wanted to go," Siros answered, without the question ever being asked.

Dhiar turned in surprise, to face the angel. "Did you...?"

"I didn't mean to. I usually don't do that. Usually I can only get little impressions. Wants, desires, things like that." Siros leaned close and kissed Dhiar's forehead. "Don't worry. Your thoughts are safe. I just saw that image so strongly... you must miss it."

Dhiar softly, slowly nodded his head. He did miss it. Even the air tasted different there. Everything was so delightful, so vivid. Every moment there truly made it feel like living. It was like everything else was just an imitation and couldn't quite get the essence.

"Would you like something to drink?" The angel moved away, gliding almost, with his wings flicking out to take him over the space.

That must be why it was so open, Dhiar thought. He likes to fly. And why shouldn't he? If one has wings, one ought to fly.

"Some juice, perhaps?"

"Pomegranate is fresh," Siros called, from the icebox. "Do you like that? I have some apple, it's a little older... the cranberry... I'm not sure if that's still any good..."

Dhiar wandered over to the area stacked high with soft pillows and blankets, undressing before he reached it. He lightly used his shirt to dry his hair a little more, then delicately draped himself along a few cushions, locks tumbling around his face, framing it like a perfect picture.

"Pomegranate, please..."

Siros nodded and reached into the icebox, pulling out the carafe and turning to take a glass. He fumbled the bottle and nearly dropped it. If not for quick reflexes, he might have.

"Sorry!" Dhiar laughed and covered his mouth. "I didn't want to get your pretty cushions wet, and my clothes are still damp from the rain and dirty from the rolling around in the garden. I hope you don't mind." He reached for one of the blankets.

"No! No, not at all." The angel grinned, pushing off the ground as he did and floating over, slipping on the air currents and touching down next to the Incubus.

He handed off the glass and started to take his own clothes off, which was a marvel to be seen. He had the most fascinating bodily hair: it was almost iridescent, like a very light blond sparkling along his body. It caught the eye, and with certain angles became more noticeable. And between the legs, what a perfectly-proportioned treat! The buttocks, how squeezable and appealing to the vision!

He settled down with Dhiar, taking the blanket and pulling it around the both of them. His arms slid around the other man, pulling him close.

"Enjoy your drink. Will you stay the night?" Then Siros caught himself and laughed. "So to speak."

"I certainly will." Dhiar sipped at the juice, pure and ruby-red. It tinted his lips.

He had intended to find somewhere to stay anyway, even if it happened to be with the host. Usually any decent party offered

accommodation for its guests who felt unable to travel home at the late hour. This, however, was a much more agreeable option.

"I love your... apartment? Condominium? I'm not sure what to call it." Dhiar leaned closer and pressed his lips to Siros's, letting him taste the fruit's sweetness left on them.

The angel just laughed, running a hand softly up and down at the small of Dhiar's back. "I'm not sure what to call it either. This place doesn't have a handy name like 'Angel's Cloud Apartments' or something like that. I just call it my place and done with it."

"It's beautiful."

"Thank you."

The Incubus leaned over the winged man to place his half-finished beverage on a low-lying table. He kept himself draped over Siros, kissing down his body, rubbing his cheek against the soft hairs. They were so soft, softer than most any Dhiar had ever felt. Clearly the angel had taken his job seriously. Every part of him was like love, good and bad, pleasant and painful... Dhiar wanted to lose himself forever in Siros, in each curve and crevasse.

Siros softly cleared his throat, bringing his hand up through the hematite curls, along his new lover's scalp. "You don't have to... you know... do anything. I'm not obligating you. We can just... I can hold you, we can sleep... there are no obligations. You don't have to do anything for me."

"I know," Dhiar quickly replied, nosing the man's navel. "I want to. I'm exploring you... I want to feel you, all over, and feel what you feel like. I want to experience you in every way... and if we take it slow, that's fine too. But I want to touch you, and smell you, and see you... taste you... hear what sounds you make... I want everything about you. I'm getting a feel for the layout, you might say."

They both laughed, the Incubus dipping his head down farther, fingers gliding along the angel's length. It was beautiful, truly. Like a pink-tipped lily, or a sceptre hewn of alabaster, kissed with the most tender tint at the very tip.

It would be a long, wonderfully long, night, he hoped.

19th Night
Foundation of Our Love

Dhiar found himself lavishing in the presence of Siros. It was easy to do. He could still taste pomegranate in his mouth, fresh pomegranate and the sweet kisses of the angel next to him, curled against him, a hand occasionally moving along his body. Dhiar kept close, an arm around the other man, careful of his delicate wings. They glistened like opals in the dim light.

The sex had all been fantastic. They had stayed in the realm of licking, touching, suckling, stroking... nothing past that, but between the two of them, it was more than enough. With so many, it always escalated so quickly to penetration of one or the other. This felt more luxurious, somehow. He always loved the feeling of exploration of another, physically and beyond.

His personal policy of keeping a healthy distance between himself and angels—more for their convenience than his—had to be looked past, this time. At least he knew up-front that Siros was not one of the uppity types.

And he was full of pleasure. Dhiar could appreciate that, as an Incubus. The place smelt strongly of Siros, but it was more a case of all his things being enhanced by his presence. The scent reminded of warmth, fresh fruits full of juices and soft fleshy pulp. It echoed sweetness and strength at the same time, not saccharine nor coming to a point, but washing softly over the senses.

The bed felt like sleeping on clouds, but it still managed to factor in as barely an accessory to the main feature that was Siros. Kind, gentle, sensual, loving, protective... and so strong. Dhiar's mind spun at the thought of it. From the garden to the place they now rested, it had been several hours. It felt like considerably less.

Dhiar smiled as he felt the warmer area between the angel's legs against his hip, the tip of the penis at the Incubus's thigh. Dhiar wiggled closer against the other man, feeling him fill softly and rise, in his sleep. Absently, he wondered if Siros were dreaming of him.

Occasionally the angel would move, the hand on Dhiar's body running over his skin and then settling in some new place. It made Dhiar smile. He couldn't decide whether to sleep, and lose himself in slumber with Siros, or to stay awake and simply bask in his presence. So he chose the latter. Demons didn't strictly need sleep very often anyway.

The Incubus lifted his hand and cupped Siros's cheek, leaning closer to him. He smelled his sweet-scented breath. It reminded him of the garden. Like a flower. He could feel the pulse between them. It felt like it rippled out eternally.

And the other man stirred, with the touch, and turned his head to kiss Dhiar's palm. It left the Incubus speechless for a time.

"Haven't you slept? I'll hold you. You can sleep." Siros wrapped his arms around Dhiar, smiling that smile of his, eyes still full of slumber and dream. "You're safe."

The Incubus leaned up and pressed against Siros, kissing his lips softly, sweetly, briefly, pulling away to rest his head under the angel's and close his eyes. The wings folded around the both of them. They put the fine bedclothes to shame. If the bed was like sleeping on clouds, being surrounded by the wings was like *being* clouds.

Silly thing. That wasn't what kept Dhiar awake. But now that the gesture had been made, he was not about to allow it to go to waste. The strong arms and soft feathers about him, the scent that naturally emanated from his lover, the slow, steady breaths, in and out... they mesmerised him into sleep. Naked body to naked body, the two sank into the velvet darkness that gave way in turn to dreams.

Hours passed unheeded, unnoticed between the two. They had no care for time, for all anyone in Noctemburg paid it attention. Some minded it for ease if they should ever go somewhere else, whereas others maintained it for appearances, for some unknowable reason. Day went to night into day, and some unknowable time later, both of the men's eyes opened, at exactly the same time.

Dhiar was the first to make a sound. Laughter issued up from his chest, and he lifted his head to brush his lips against Siros's. He slid his hands up the angel's sides, over his nipples, to rest in the centre of his chest.

"See? Wasn't that wonderful sleep?" Siros answered the kiss with one of his own, rubbing his lips against Dhiar's, suckling on one, nipping at the other, barely teasing with the dance of his tongue. "You don't have to worry about anything when you're here with me."

The Incubus only kept laughing, almost collapsing against Siros. "You're so delightfully silly," he answered. "I wasn't worried... but I don't think I've ever felt so warm and welcome as I have in your arms." Another kiss, and then he took a breath to continue. "Sleeping—actual sleeping—with someone else next to you, that takes trust and beauty. You gave me such beautiful dreams."

Dhiar stroked his fingers through Siros's hair, feeling its softness, its thick and healthy lustre. The angel traced around a small horn with his thumb.

"I didn't give them to you," Siros replied. "We crafted them as one."

Dhiar reflected at that moment that it should not surprise him that an angel is such a perfectly ideal lover. In many ways, he thought, they were much the same: beings of pleasure and happiness. Not all of the angels were like that, of course. But this one, this one was special. He seemed almost like the good angel archetype, brightness and comfort and love exuded from every fibre of his being.

The Incubus bent slightly closer, reaching his hand down, and he cupped Siros between the legs, stroking over his balls and then up the erection that had fully settled in whilst they slept. Yes, that was an especially appealing feature. So many of the more uppity angels tried to deny they even had anything between the legs. But this one, this one celebrated it. And Dhiar could see himself finding plenty of time to worship it.

"Good morning to you too!" Dhiar murmured, barely able to stop himself from giggling.

Siros erupted in a sudden burst of laughter, quieting to start rocking his hips against the soft fingers touching him so.

"Good morning to you." He leaned in for another kiss.

20th Night
I'm So Sorry Baby

"I probably don't have to tell you," Dhiar started, playing his fingers along Siros's chest, "but I don't tend to let myself get entangled with angels."

"Oh!" Siros took Dhiar's hand by the wrist and brought it up to his lips, kissing it. "If you want me to go, I—"

The hand wriggled away and the Incubus pressed his fingers to Siros's mouth. "Shush. What I was going to say was that I typically don't let myself get entangled with angels, because so many of them here are so vastly inferior to the dream-come-true I happen to be faced with right now." He grinned, leaning up to replace his fingers with his lips. "Siros, the last few days have been like a fantasy. I keep thinking I'll wake up in my shop and it'll have all been some kind of cruel dream."

The angel smiled and matched the kiss, breathing out softly against Dhiar's face. "When I sensed your aura, I knew you were as kind and gentle as you've shown me. I have heard of you... I never thought I would have the good fortune to be the recipient of your good graces."

Dhiar just stared up into those eyes. He had lost himself, so many times, in their sparkling depths. No matter what the light, they happened to catch it. No matter where he was, no matter where he looked, if he wanted to catch them, he would.

"You were interested in me? You knew of me?"

"Of course!" Siros brushed the back of his fingers under the demon's jaw, over his chin and back again. "I know several people in the city who go to your shop all the time. It's truly a unique locale in this city. Something the city needs, in my opinion."

"Well. Thank you." Dhiar had no idea what else to say. Someone had heard of him! He usually just consumed himself with work, with the day-to-day running of the shop and its products. His mind raced to think of whom these friends might be.

He completely blanked his thoughts when he felt Siros kissing him again. His lashes fluttered, his heart thumped, and his breath caught in his throat.

The two drifted back to the floor, to the carpets covering most of the place. Either there were carpets or cushions, usually both, and that had led to days simply relaxing together, basking in their new love.

As such, neither had worn clothes since they removed them from the rain. The excuse was that they needed time to dry, although by now they could probably have used a wash. Dhiar didn't care. He was too busy occupying himself tasting Siros and his soft, sweet lips. He loved how they mingled with the taste of pomegranate; that first night had left him with an influence, a fixation. The taste turned his mind upside-down, all mingled together.

But Siros went well with a variety of fruits. Dhiar had personally tried every single type of juice he had in the icebox. It was almost to the point where they might actually have to go out to get more... he sighed and nuzzled up, pressing lips to lips again.

He could feel his penis filling, and what's more, he could feel Siros growing hard against him. They had almost the same size, and it delighted Dhiar every time he beheld it. The soft skin rubbed against his. He fought back a moan halfway, turning it into a persistent hum that vibrated all through his chest.

A little wetness, a little stickiness began to mingle between them. Another series of kisses, something to lose himself in. Dhiar slowly licked along the angel's jaw. He slipped his hand down and grabbed a buttock, feeling it, feeling it give, the softness, the flex of the muscle afterwards, the pulse of tension.

Siros took in a sudden breath, arching his back and pressing his chest against Dhiar's. It would not be long now. Surely not long now. His wings curled around the both of them in an embrace, soft, fluffy, feathery-downy. More luxurious than any bird's feathers were these. They smelled like flying. Just like flying.

Now the Incubus nibbled on his ear, running his fingers up

the curve of his back. He would not force it, he would not rush it... it was there to be savored. His breath tickled hot against Siros's cheek. Their hearts beat as one.

It continued to rise around him. To Dhiar, it was like composing a symphony of two, that union, that connection, merging together, melding naturally, feeling himself be lost for even a moment in another. When they mingled and touched in nature, in being, in essence, it all came to its climax. He could feel himself release at the same time as Siros, hot and sticky and wonderful. The angel's wings stretched out far above them, almost touching the overhang.

And then the denouement. Everything slowed gradually. Dhiar could feel the stars float down around him, the same stars that had sparkled in his sight as his body answered. He still felt like he was floating. Every time, just like flight.

Then it occurred to him.

"Hey." Dhiar kissed delicately at Siros's face, the angel glowing as he wordlessly attempted to resolve the feelings echoing in his body. "Would you, um, ever consider taking me flying? I mean... I don't want to impose, of course, but you know..."

For a few seconds, Siros could not answer. Every time, every time with Dhiar, it rendered him speechless. He nuzzled at the Incubus's cheek, catching his breath and lowering his body atop the other man.

"Mm, yes. I will fly with you any time you wish it." He placed another kiss on Dhiar's lips. "My sweet love."

The Incubus's reddish cheeks turned a shade deeper pink, and he turned his head to catch Siros, to kiss him in return before he retreated too far. "Sweet love? You're kind. Too kind." Raising a hand, he combed through the dark-to-light locks. "You're much sweeter than me."

"We can discuss it in the air," Siros replied, pulling up to his feet and offering a hand up, with a smile. "After we wash off a little bit."

21st Night
Shadows of the Night

"You know, you really don't have to if you don't want to." Dhiar reclined against Siros in the coach.

It was horse-drawn, but by no horses known to the dwellers of the surface; no, these were special steeds, just as the ones in Lothring's place. Though these seemed much more lively. They simply were of the same stock as the vampires, the throngs of undead who had forged ahead into the uncertain darkness and made Noctemburg what it had become.

Dhiar liked the cabs. He was never really a huge fan of automobiles. He wasn't good at driving them, though Chana seemed to like them. Siros's presence made everything better, though.

The angel played his fingers upon Dhiar's chest, smiling down at him. "Of course I want to. I asked to."

This part of the trip always made his home seem more foreboding than it strictly had any business presenting itself. The shadows stretched, tall and long, on either side of the street. It always seemed as if, no matter what the time of day, whenever one vehicle clattered down the path, nothing else was within earshot. Everything went perfectly quiet, aside from hoof-beats and the turning of wooden wheels on stone.

But then it was past, and the lights of his home came through the windows. There were little curtains on the windows, though Dhiar had no need to draw them. The lights here ranged from warm, welcoming colours to lurid and neon, piercing the darkness with a bawdy cry of "notice me!" The club across the street always seemed much the latter, and try as Dhiar might, he could not settle himself into accepting too much neon for his own shop.

The distinctness, at least, set him apart from the nearby businesses. Whatever his opinions of the lights, they seemed to work for him. What crowds went to the club were drawn in by their own illuminations.

The cab came to a stop, and the door opened from the outside. Dhiar shifted to his feet and pulled Siros up, smiling to him and squeezing his hands in the angel's. He leaned in for a soft little kiss before stepping down the little stairs provided by the footman.

After a handsome tip, the cab was off again, leaving the two before the shop. It wasn't particularly lofty, just two floors and a roof terrace. It blended in as it could, but something about it stood out regardless. Dhiar watched Siros, a bit nervous that perhaps his new lover might actually dislike his home. Perhaps he would disapprove.

But the Incubus lived his own life, as always. If that was that, then so be it. He waved his hand to the door. "Would you like to come in? I live upstairs. The shop's downstairs."

"Please!" Siros all but launched himself at the door.

Dhiar laughed lightly to himself, a bit surprised. He pulled the door open, never having to worry about it. The shop knew him. It opened for him, and only him, when he wanted it to do so. "After you."

Siros glided into Phantasies, eyes wide at the surroundings, at the accoutrements, all the décor... it almost overwhelmed him. On every note, he found it complementary to his own tastes. A smile, then a grin, slowly curled his lips, and he reached his arms to pull Dhiar against him.

"It's marvellous," he murmured, kissing the top of the Incubus's head. "Better than I had even dreamt. It's like I've been away from home and just arrived back after a long time."

Dhiar closed his eyes, turning his head to kiss Siros's chest, taking in the sweetness of his skin. "Welcome home."

The angel rubbed his hand along Dhiar's arm. "Will you show me your home? I mean, your living area? The shop is so wonderful... I can only imagine what that is like."

"Of course!" Dhiar moved to the counter with the register, taking Siros by the hand and leading him behind the silk screen.

Through the doorway, up the stairs, past the posters papering the stairwell with naked, cheerful men, they went. Up to the little platform in front of the loft's door, where Dhiar stepped out of his boots and helped Siros up with his soft shoes. Then they continued inside together, pressed close. Siros huddled his wings around the both of them.

He took in a deep breath suddenly, upon being inside the loft. Everything about it felt right. It felt like Dhiar, like holding him all night, being held by him.

The Incubus raised his eyebrows expectantly.

"It's beautiful," Siros answered, to the unspoken enquiry. "No, it's more than that, but I don't know a word to describe it. It's wonderful! It's... you. It's so very you. It's like being a part of you, being inside you... in a sense," he hastily amended, cheeks going pink.

Dhiar only laughed so softly, placing one hand upon each cheek and gazing deep into his eyes, into those opal pools. Every bit of light twinkled and sparkled, iridescent, reflecting back into his own dark gaze.

"All you have to do is say the word." The Incubus winked and kissed Siros again, before pulling back and drifting kitchen-ward.

It was almost addictive, kissing Siros. The angel had not been misleading about his previous occupation under a love-god. He had to have been. It was like Siros were simply a different kind of Incubus, well-versed and breathtaking in the ways of pleasure and affection.

He was, in many ways, an ideal lover and partner in intimacy. And so earnest! Dhiar had rarely had such a combination of experience and earnest innocence. They had still not intruded within each other. Dhiar could not resolve it with the feelings of the moment yet. It was still not time. Even if the comment enticed him, even if he desired it...

He glanced to Siros, who looked up and met his gaze instantly. It sent a shiver down his back. Dhiar's eyelids lowered a bit more, his lips parted, and he felt almost touched in his most private of places.

Tonight... he would have Siros's arms around him, in his own bed, and that would be enough.

22nd Night
Rocket's Tail

The air in the bathroom had a substance to it, heavy and full. The steam from the hot bath rose, scented with vanilla and rose petals, the same petals drifting about the surface of the water in the garden tub. The water held the appearance of glass, until movement from one figure or the other disturbed it. Ripples rolled out like reflections from one side to the other.

It was cold outside, but not yet the bitter cold of winter. It made the skylight steam up, opaque and not so playful as in warmer weather. It looked like frosted glass.

Dhiar's toes played along the side of Siros's thigh. The angel's wings stretched out around the side of the tub, curled along its curve, covered with the sparkling iridescence of tiny rivulets of moisture. He slightly spread his legs, and even through the distorting movement of water, it was easy to see what he offered, half-floating, half-pointing to Dhiar.

The hairs on Siros's body showed more easily, with the wetness of the bath. Dhiar's were visible most of the rest of the time anyway, with his dark features. A veritable arrow pointed between his legs, a trail under his arms, while Siros had a more subtle series of designs directing the eyes to certain features.

Slowly their breathing would match, in pace, and then it would desynchronise again. The detail amused them. Dhiar slid his foot up, over Siros's leg, and between them. He curled his toes in the hair for a moment, then drew the side of his toe up the side of the angel's length. It responded as expected, growing, filling, becoming fuller.

Siros closed his eyes and arched his back, muscles tensing and showing, so well-defined with the heat and the wetness, rivulets beading and trickling over the gentle curves of his body. It was already hot in the bathroom. Now it felt like a steam bath.

The sultry vapours rose, vanilla and rose petal joined with the inimitable and unmistakable scent of arousal. Dhiar could feel it, as he shared the sensations through touch and closeness. He augmented it, accenting it, feeding it back to his lover and feeling the reaction. Between his own legs, he grew stiff and tall.

The Incubus moved his foot up and down, sliding the angel's length between two toes. His own leg flexed. The muscles glistened, tight and so visible. Dhiar started to grin, looking from Siros's feet, up his sturdy legs, between them, over his navel, the contours of his stomach, over his chest, the depression at his collar, the wiry stock of his neck, and over his strong jaw. His face, his lips, his nose, his eyes... he kept losing himself in them, as bright as his own were dark.

The sky outside remained shadowed as ever. He wondered how it must look in the world above. He could recall the days of autumn, all the colours, the foliage, yet things were different, underground. The trees and flowers and all the plants still bloomed and bore leaves and fruit, but a different fruit entirely from those above. No moody autumn skies loomed over, no afternoons filled with dreams of floating away above the fiery maple treetops in a hot-air balloon.

No sweetness of the decaying autumn leaves, or the bittersweetness of their burning on the air, roasting chestnuts or sweet potatoes in the smouldering remains. These things, too, were undeniably sensual, undeniably pleasures, and yet here, in the underground, they were all but unseen. So few here had time or inclination to do so. Even in Lothring's place, they only observed the leaves as they went to dust and plastered the ground like so much papier-mâché.

It was always the little things that added accents. It was the little things one missed, when one went without.

Dhiar curled his toes again, squeezing at the tip. Siros could not help himself. The water suddenly became cloudy, and he let out a soft little sound that echoed around the room as if he had cried out.

Suddenly the Incubus found himself reclined against the side of the bath, his body half-lifted, Siros gazing intently into his eyes. One hand pumped the Incubus's erection, the other toyed with his entrance and then, without much waiting, penetrated past the muscle and inside. It took little doing for him to find the best spot, but before he got too far, it became clear that Incubi had many, many pleasure spots; they were practically lined with them.

The pulses rang intensely from Dhiar's psyche, and he almost lost control of them entirely in surprise. He leaned up to take Siros's mouth with his own, tongues tangling for a moment and then retreating, to let the lips do their more important work. His body brimmed over with sensation. It made his skin tingle, goose-flesh rising on him. He moaned louder than the angel had, and it sounded even more mighty an utterance, echoing about the room, reverberating off the water's surface and the tile.

The Incubus could barely control himself anymore. Siros drove him mad. And the angel felt himself spiralling out of control as well, with Dhiar unable to hold back as much of the sharing of sensation, the emphasis of pleasure, as he had before. He felt himself overstimulated, beyond reason, and without even rising to full erection, full enough to curve up slightly, he came again. At the same time, Dhiar clenched around his intruding fingers and shot his nectar up, up over his chest, onto his body, onto his face.

He panted, writhing still in ecstasy, ready to continue and yet completely unprepared to do so. Siros kept stroking dumbly, as if stunned by all of the release and its feelings. Dhiar shivered, all over his body. He could feel himself washed with warmth, his body tingling with numbness, all up and down, to his fingertips. If he weren't already soaked, he surely would have been shortly. Sweatdrops tickled his cheeks and neck.

With the sound of flowing in the air, the sound of water moving, the scent of intense pleasure hanging around them, Dhiar smiled as he looked into Siros's eyes. He could see the delight of everything in them.

He had conceived an idea.

23rd Night
Time of the Season

The sun shining down on them was as different as could be from Noctemburg's perpetual night. At first it hurt Dhiar's eyes a little bit, to be so bright. But even it was not as oppressively bright as it could have been.

There, in the subterranean grandeur of Dis, the Great City of the Abyss... there, the place which Dhiar had known for so much of his youth, which all of his kind know and had known... the trees grew taller than buildings, the streets cobbled and the buildings a mixture of the most beautiful of designs.

In this place, Siros felt completely awed. It was a bit like Dhiar felt around Siros, like this other person, this splendid other person in his life, had such power and knowledge, such a natural awareness of things that he himself could not. In this place, he could stretch his wings. He could fly, and fly into a sky; despite being underground, the Abyss actually had a sky, celestial bodies, and other things that seemed like luxuries by comparison to Noctemburg.

In autumn, of course, the vast trees rained down leaves of all colours on the city. It looked like a city afire, as the leaves twirled and floated down, like a kind of snow. Siros could imagine that in spring, the blossoms of some of the trees probably made a closer resemblance, with white and sugar pink.

"Isn't it marvellous?" Dhiar called over his shoulder. "I thought, enough with rolling it over in my mind! I should go back, even if only for a little while. And you had wanted to go, so..."

"Oh yes," Siros replied. "It's amazing." He hurried to catch up to the Incubus, flapping his wings and gliding along the broad street. "Were you born here?"

Dhiar pursed his lips thoughtfully, before making his answer. "Not exactly," came the unhelpful reply. "Oh! The Cathédrale du Thé!"

Frenetically the Incubus pointed down a side street. "Hurry! Let's go that way. You can make it faster... carry me?"

"The... the what?" Siros held out his arms, for Dhiar to make himself comfortable.

Dhiar climbed up, wrapping his arms about Siros's neck and resting his head on the man's shoulder. "The Cathédrale du Thé. It's a cathedral, you see, and they serve tea, coffee, and things like that. It's wonderful. Probably the most popular of such destinations in the Abyss. Come, come, just down that way and up the larger street where it opens."

By the instructions given, the winged man hurtled into the air and over the buildings making up the block. His eyes could see it as he reached the air: a vast structure, stretching up, up, with spires and flying buttresses, and so many touches that staggered the imagination. Stained glass gleamed as the sunlight caught it, and he could only dream, for the moment, of the shapes and colours it cast within. All of these things seemed to celebrate the delight and glory of tea, in all its forms.

They set down at the front, near the steps and inclines, and made their way in the giant doorway. Doors in the Great City rarely ever closed, at least in the case of large places like this. The most public of landmarks, how could they ever? At all hours of the long day and night, there stood the Cathédrale, welcoming one and all to its aromatic insides.

Siros slowly took in a breath, setting Dhiar down but keeping his arms around the Incubus. "It's..." He simply trailed off, leaning his head against Dhiar's and closing his eyes for a moment, to let his sense of smell take precedence.

"Isn't it?" Dhiar chuckled, knowing the meaning, even if the words remained unspoken. "I'm glad to take you of all people here. You really can appreciate it. And of course, I can appreciate the company."

Reaching up, the Incubus stroked the back of Siros's hand, and the angel opened his eyes. His smile slowly spread, and he turned to kiss Dhiar's ear. "Mm. Let's get some tea."

They made their way to the counter. There must have been a

hundred jars behind it, if there were one. Baked goods and sweets of all kinds were listed on the menu, and a few of them stood in the display. The people behind the counter were every bit as interesting and notable as the rest of Dis's inhabitants, each bearing a certain unique quality that set him apart from everyone else.

The most important difference, Siros reflected, in the Great City, in the Cathédrale, and the rest of the worlds that Siros had seen, was the fact that the people here who worked in these places did so because they wanted to do so. They loved them. And the people who came recognised that and were there, likewise, because they wanted to be. It was a remarkable dynamic: so simple, and yet so perfectly reasonable.

It seemed no time at all before the two of them sat at one of the tables a little higher up, looking down on the main floor, near the largest stained glass in the place. The inside of the Cathédrale looked a kaleidoscope to his eyes, ever-thrilling and stimulating with all the colours of innocent delight.

Siros pulled his chair closer to Dhiar's, leaning over to kiss the corner of his mouth. "Tea goes best with kisses," he murmured to the Incubus. "I don't know if you were aware."

Dhiar turned to press his mouth full against the angel's, closing his eyes and running a hand through his hair. "Mm... I've always said so," he replied softly, pulling back and gazing intently into his eyes. "So... do you like the Great City?"

"I love it!" Siros laughed, sitting back in his chair and reaching out to take up his cup of vanilla chai. "I couldn't ask for something more marvellous. It's one of the most... it's the perfect city for me, I have to say."

Dhiar nodded his head, eyes twinkling as they never did in Noctemburg. "Even if it's only for a little while, I think we can enjoy our time here. Anything is more valuable, more appreciable, when one doesn't have it. We'll whet our appetites here and then, well... then we'll be happy wherever we go, for our memories."

Siros lifted his cup in a sort of salute, as if making a toast. "Memories!" He echoed.

24th Night
Hounds of Love

The days were so luxuriously long, the nights seemed endless, and all in all Dhiar was having a great time. It felt so good to go home, even once in a while. The time that passed between the occasions made it seem all the more special.

And now, arm-in-arm with Siros, he walked down the streets of stone towards the sound of music and the glow of lights.

This music pulsed and writhed through the body, it pulled one's very being into rhythm. Even if a person had never danced, it made them want to move. They might not know a pirouette from a fox-trot, but this was the kind of sound where it all became so magnificently irrelevant. This was not the time for well-learned, practised motion.

As the two passed through the doorway, Dhiar motioned to the sight that greeted them. A huge column of what looked like solid water stretched up from a pool. Lush flora surrounded the walk, with seats and tables closer to the intermittent running walls and plant life, away from the main dance floor... which seemed to be mainly in the water, with a few floating platforms just adjacent to it.

Doorways led off to the buildings, exotic arches draped with diaphanous curtains. The bottles and glasses behind bars glimmered from the opposite curves of the place's design. People of all kinds milled about, more naked than dressed.

"The Pit!" Dhiar proclaimed. "The greatest club of the Great City, in the eyes of many. The water there, don't worry about that, you can breathe in it. And the doors lead off to... lounges. For relaxation."

By Dhiar's tone, Siros knew at once exactly what kind of relaxation he had in mind. The angel reached down to adjust himself in his trousers, only partially succeeding before Dhiar enthusiastically tugged him in the direction of the liquid pillar.

The Incubus wasted no time pulling him inside, and it was then that Siros completely understood the appeal of the Pit and its main attraction: the sounds were different, of course, inside: as pervasive as the beat had been outside, it was as if the music could only fully be experienced within the water. It hummed and thumped all through his body, and it rushed all around. He felt clothed by the music. His body could not resist.

Dhiar was part of the music. He stripped off his shirt and let it float away, rubbing his chest against Siros's, pressing up against him. No sweat, no tension of the muscles, could exist here. Bubbles fluttered from his mouth as he blew a kiss, then leaned up to press mouth to mouth.

Siros's clothes clung to his form, wet and pressed in by his surroundings. He shivered for a moment, then leaned into the kiss. As he drifted with Dhiar, moving constantly, he could see the others around them. So many were naked, which made sense with the water. Why not feel it all around one's entire body?

Erections were worn without shame, and openly, freely. He could not help his eyes settling on a choice couple, as they rubbed against their partners and then waved free, side to side. The little floating hairs formed shapes on the body like arrows to guide the eyes. He almost could not look away.

But Dhiar quickly fixed that, too. The Incubus let his hands wander down, pushing Siros's trousers to his knees, pulling at a foot and pulling him floating horizontally. The angel looked down his body in surprise and then delight, watching as his own penis jutted up, almost as a metronome for Dhiar's symphony.

And what a symphony it was! Those lips replaced the water and sucked on the angel, and soon the Incubus himself drifted around, kicking his own pants away, wearing only a pair of boots. His cock beckoned to Siros, and so the winged man leaned up to accommodate, licking at its tip and then taking it to suck on at once.

They continued to drift, like a kind of ouroboros in the open, deep space. No-one tried to shame them, no-one called out in shock. There was only pleasure, and an acceptance of its enjoyment. This place was a collection of pleasure, after all. What great joys it offered! Surrounded by music so great that it completely saturated the body, mind and spirit, to share with another only made it more pleasureable.

Siros came about the same time as Dhiar, a few pearly strands drifting around them as they separated slightly. Then the Incubus wrapped his legs around Siros's waist and started to stroke him again, bringing him back up and pushing back on him. The angel tried to voice a concern for his lover, but it felt too good... and the water completely obscured any sound he could make. It wasn't part of the composition.

He drove into Dhiar, the motions creating a kind of easy rush of the water around them. Both men's hair drifted about their heads like tendrils, flowering vines made of some kind of jewel. It was paradise. Utter bliss! He had never openly fucked anyone on a dance floor, in the middle of a club. But the realisation excited him still more.

Dhiar arched his back, the muscles more fully supported and enhanced in appearance by the water around them. He flexed and clenched, and then suddenly white wisps rose like smoky clouds from between his legs. And almost in a sort of triumph, Siros reached climax after him, humming to himself, feeling the vibration resonant around his body and complemented by the instruments sounding throughout their world at that moment.

It was minutes before either of them managed to move much more on his own. At last, Siros wrapped Dhiar in his arms and pushed to the edge, gliding down to the pool to relax in the open air. The atmosphere was so different, without the music completely there. He couldn't feel it as much anymore; neither of them could. But in some ways, it was also a relief. They would have to rest, recover their energy, and then...

Dhiar grinned up at Siros, rubbing back against his body.

25th Night
Tsumetai Tsuki

The night pressed on. By now, Siros wanted rest, and so he slept in the room they shared. But as often happened in the night, Dhiar found himself restless, and so he picked himself up and took himself for a walk.

He couldn't remember how long he had walked, or the turns he had taken; it didn't matter, in Dis. He would find his way back easily enough when he wanted to return.

The air was crisp around him. The Moon glowed in the sky, looking down on the city and all within. Dhiar slid his hands inside his long red coat and smiled as he met that gaze with his own, enchanted by the celestial sphere which seemed to hop whimsically back and forth between silver and gold.

The scent of snow, for only a moment, tingled in his nostrils. He knew at once where he needed to go.

And so, after a moment, he found himself in one of the many train stations, and then on a train. It wouldn't take long. He knew just the place. It had been ages since he visited last, but one of the most marvellous things about his home was that things always tended to be there, even if they had changed a little bit.

This place, however, had changed hardly at all. It was still a country house, with a vast, sloping roof. Dhiar smiled as he stepped in and felt the heat from the hearth, set in the middle of the floor. It always felt like somewhere one could call home. It reminded him of the time he spent in Hokkaidou.

A few people sat at tables in the place, but he imagined he probably had missed the real rush of the day. A voice rang out from behind him, and he turned.

"Welcome back."

His eyes settled onto the form of a man who at once seemed young and old, dressed in old clothes. They had once been new and colourful, but now they looked a little tired. It suited the man, though; if he had wanted new ones, it would have been an easy affair in the city. These were kept because they had some meaning to him.

Dhiar beamed, taking in a breath. "Hanchi!"

"Hanbei while we're here," the man corrected, laughing nonetheless. "I kid. Where's life been keeping you?" He placed his hand on Dhiar's shoulder, guiding him to one of the places to sit. "I haven't seen you in... what probably is a very long time, anywhere else."

"Oh, well... Noctemburg, but I had to get away for a while. We're staying in the city, I decided to play tour guide."

"You left your guest in the city while you flitted up here? Well, maybe you'll relent later and bring me another guest." Hanbei sat with Dhiar. He waved to catch the attention of a younger woman and mouthed silent words across the room, making hand gestures.

Dhiar rather luxuriously draped himself along the cushions supposed to be seats. He liked to think he didn't need as much rest. Maybe he wanted it, he reflected. He wasn't sure.

"I don't know," he replied at last. "I don't know if this is his kind of place."

"Only one way to find out. Sit up, I don't want you choking." Hanbei nodded to the girl, as she brought a large ceramic carafe and two wooden cups. He poured one full, and Dhiar sat up and poured the other.

"Kanpai!" The Incubus raised his cup cheerfully, saluting the other man, and the two drank at the same time. "Ahh... it's so beautiful..." His words faded as his eyes caught the Moon again, this time through the wide window in the roof.

Hanbei slowly turned to see. A smile slowly unfolded across his soft features. "He is cold tonight," he quietly remarked, nearly a whisper. He took another drink.

"The Moon?"

"Mm." Hanbei nodded once, setting his cup down. "If it weren't so cool, I'd say we should go outside and catch his reflection in the sake. It makes it taste better."

"It's not that cold."

Hanbei looked over at the man across the low table from him, and he couldn't help but match the grin. With his expression, the thick, bushy mop of black on his head gave him such a boyish appearance. A few minutes later, they sat outside on the grass.

It still felt warm enough, although the temperature never really affected Dhiar. Hanbei seemed at least comfortable, in the coat he had pulled on over his regular clothes.

"It's easier with the big, wide cups," Hanbei explained. "A little harder with these. But worth it."

Dhiar looked into his fresh drink, lowering it, angling it... and then he smiled again, seeing that almost blue image glistening silver along the ripples of his clear drink. Its faintly nutty aroma rose, steam curling in the cool of the night. Even with the murmurings of conversation inside the large house, the village around them sat all but silent.

That silence always seemed to come just before a snow. The clouds had begun to gather, low and dark and thick. They, too, danced on the surface of the glassy sake.

"So you're in Noctemburg now, are you?" The young-old man nursed his drink, leaning back on a hand. "I've heard that's quite a place to live."

Dhiar rolled his shoulders back. "I'm not sure how much longer I'll be there." His tone held a kind of sadness, but within it lingered a resolve. "It was once the only place for me. I couldn't imagine finding a place better to live, outside of the Great City. But now..."

"Now you've made too many memories for it to stay that way?"

"Something like that."

"Ahh. That's how it is."

The conversation continued easily, comfortably, as they finished the carafe. A little unsurely, Dhiar got to his feet and gave his best grin, which at the moment was lopsided and drunken.

"If I bring him tomorrow, can you make nabemono? A nice big hot pot. With all the vegetables, the little dumplings, and..."

"If you bring him tomorrow, we'll have a great nabemono." Hanbei laughed and clapped Dhiar's shoulder. "But if you don't get back to him now, you won't be awake tomorrow."

The two laughed together. They walked back to the door of the house and then embraced, a tight, affectionate hug, leaning into each other.

Hanbei leaned back, then, and against the door frame. "But even if you don't make it here tomorrow, I was glad to see you."

"Me too." Dhiar wobbled a step back. "I mean... glad to see you. Always."

"Take care of yourself."

"And you."

Then Dhiar was alone again. He pushed his hands into his pockets, still warmed by the drink, and started along the path back to the train station.

Looking skyward, he let his eyes reflect the Moon, one more time.

26th Night
Eden

Dhiar contemplated the sleeping man. Siros presented even more of an pure portrait as he slept. His bare chest rose and fell so softly, his lashes moved slightly every so often, and his wings lightly fluttered with them.

He closed his eyes again and pressed against the angel's side, breathing deeply and slowly. His journey into night had been long, and he hoped sleep would take him soon. It always seemed easier in Dis. The dreams somehow always seemed like they were closer, almost enough to touch at any moment in time.

His body fit so well against Siros, two naked forms together. His penis had lazily filled halfway and pressed against the other man's hip, and the smoulder of desire remained. Casually, Dhiar curled and reached his hand down to feel Siros, to see if he matched it; his fingers brushed over an almost full erection.

A little moan escaped the angel's lips. Dhiar smiled to himself and slowly stroked his darling, eyes still closed. His sense of touch would be given precedence now. The feeling emanated from him, and he shared his sensation. He wondered how it might influence Siros's dreams. Hopefully, he thought, it would make them sweeter.

Drawing his fingertips to the head, he stroked only there for a time. He could feel himself rising to full mast, and his hips started to move, almost on their own. The soft skin of the winged man felt so magnificently wonderful on the soft skin of his length. He could not decide which managed to be silkier, of the two.

The pad of his thumb rubbed over the other man's slit, parting the two sides for only an instant. He spread the slick wetness around the tip, smiling to himself. So many delights derived from this singular part, and its appearance and shape all suggested an awareness of how superbly it presented itself to the hand. Not necessarily a handle, he reflected, but a highly entertaining spot for hands to go.

The angel really fascinated him. It had been so long since Dhiar had afforded himself the luxury of really falling for one, and this one seemed hewn from the stuff of his dreams. He never tried to deny the fact that, quite naturally, he loved cocks, admired them, and was enthralled at everything about them. He was a connoisseur of cocks, anyone who knew him would say so. But when it was love, and deep love as well, for the person to whom said cock was attached, it became a sort of singular mindfulness.

He loved the light curve to it, when it was completely and utterly full, the angle which pointed back to the body, up to the navel. There was the so-soft nest of hair around the base that he loved to press his face against and inhale. And the marvellous, pendulous balls beneath, always seeming so full and well-crafted as he rolled them along his fingers.

Even when he didn't mean to arouse, he found himself wanting to touch it, to be near it, however he could. He held it if Siros let him, when he urinated. The way it sprang to life and hummed with rushing liquid gave such pleasure to his fingers. It brought a bit of a wicked grin to the Incubus's face as he lay there thinking of it, slowly continuing his attention to the sleeping angel.

There were other especially pleasing areas, ones that Dhiar could not get out of his mind. The downy hair under Siros's arms always had a pleasant, clean, deep scent about it, and it felt ever soft and lush against his bare cheek. The man's nipples were, in a word, luxurious, if any nipples could be called such. His buttocks dipped and rose in just the way they ought, for his body, and between them the most insouciant and pert little bud rested. Dhiar had only rarely even touched it, thus far in their relationship. But how he longed to do more to it! How he longed to explore every inch of Siros, outside and in as far as he could imagine it.

He could not help himself; his fingers ventured there, caressing it lightly, and back up the underside, between the legs, over the balls and to the very tip of the penis. And then, as quickly as that, he felt a warm, sticky wetness cover his fingers, and pressed insistently to Siros's hip.

With that slightest gesture, he released his own, to join it. The angel murmured and turned to take Dhiar in his arms, kissing the top of his head.

The Incubus grinned catlike and pressed against Siros's chest, feeling the thump of his heart and the comforting buzz of the power intrinsic to him. The utter silence and darkness made it all the more velvety, in their pleasing warm web, kept perfectly so by their nearness and the soft bedclothes around them.

After a handful of minutes, Siros licked and smacked his lips, leaning up for another kiss, to Dhiar's forehead.

"Dhiar," he murmured, voice cracking with sleep.

The Incubus marvelled at him, leaning in to kiss his lips sweetly, then lingering for a moment longer, then a moment more from that. He also loved the angel's mouth. His lips tasted of ambrosia.

At last, he forced himself to calm and quietly resigned to a nuzzle. "Yes?"

"Could you, er... bring me the chamberpot?"

Dhiar began to grin again, showing his lovely pearly teeth. "Could anyone do any less for his lover? But you mustn't move." He stroked the man's hip. "I must have you that way."

He slipped away from Siros and across the room, wetting a cloth in the basin and taking it too. As he drew the covers back again, he reached down to clean Siros and then himself, restoring the skin to its supple beauty.

"That way, eh?" Siros took a deep breath, battling the urge to rise again.

Dhiar nodded his head and reached between Siros's legs, sliding the pot under his penis and aiming at an angle downward. "And I get to hold it."

"Fair enough." The angel's eyes gleamed in the dark room. "But when you have to go, I'm going to insist on doing the same to you."

Dhiar's eyebrows shot up, and in that instant the pot began to fill.

27th Night
Where You Are

Dhiar reclined on his chaise lounge, sipping some slushy drink that seemed less and less frosty with every passing moment.

"You know, I'm not really a beach person, but I really do like it here." He adjusted the sunglasses on his face. "It's so... 'my pace'. You know?"

Beside him, lying on a large towel on the sand, Siros stretched out wings and arms with a steadily-spreading smile. "You mean like... taking things at your own measure? Taking them as they come? Yes... it seems that way." He looked up at the sky, then at the crashing water, wave after wave tumbling in. "It's remarkable that it could be so warm here and so cool in the rest of the city..."

The Incubus rolled his shoulders back, reaching up with his free hand to scratch at the centre of his bare chest. "Yes, well... that's a part of the Abyss too. You can go one place and it's almost always in one season, and another place will be in another. Sometimes they're always in one season, aside from a few special occasions... fortunately, the public transportation is awfully good, isn't it?"

Siros laughed and nodded his head, pushing himself to sit up and reaching over to rummage in the cooler they had brought. "Do you have any more of that drink? I could do with a cool-off..."

Dhiar sat his glass down and leaned over to assist, producing a chilled glass and pouring it full of the stuff, from a thick bottle. The cooler was immense, and in it they had packed enough food and drink to last easily the entire rest of the afternoon.

"Thanks!" Siros lifted his drink and sipped at it. "So why did you insist on wearing those silly trunks?" The angel, of course, was completely naked, body oiled and gleaming with the sunlight playing upon his muscles. "Isn't it hotter that way?"

Dhiar clicked his tongue, returning the curly straw between his lips for a refreshing gulp of his own. "Clothes are funnest when you have the thrill of taking them off. Or... having them taken off by someone special."

Siros's brows shot up, eyes widening, and then his eyelids lowered as he leaned along the side of Dhiar's chair. "Oh *really* now..."

"Really!" Dhiar tapped the tip of his finger to the tip of the angel's nose.

"So is that why you haven't been swimming yet?"

"One of several reasons!" Dhiar softly laughed, setting his drink on the top of the cooler. "But I could likely be persuaded."

Siros placed his beside the other glass and hopped to his feet, wings fluttering. "Let's have a dip!"

The Incubus curled forward and stepped onto the sand, wiggling his toes in it. "Yes, let's—"

The thought went without completion as Siros quickly leaned over and yanked Dhiar's shorts to his knees, sending the demon's cock bouncing in the sea breeze. With a powerful burst of his wings, the angel was airborne before Dhiar had even an instant to react. Both of them burst into laughter.

Without any concern, the Incubus stepped calmly out of his trunks and raced to the water, reaching in and splashing up at the circling winged man. Siros descended in a spiral and scooped Dhiar into his arms, bringing him close for a kiss, lingering for a while in it.

The taste of those lips, sweetened by the fruit drink, given a salty contrast by the water around them... it made an utterly delectable treat. And two bodies rubbed close against each other, slippery with the water, yet with something of a grit in it, for it was salt water of course, like any beach. The scent in the air surrounded them with freshness and the inimitable vitality of the sea.

Siros caught himself, retreating from the kiss with a self-conscious little laugh and running his hand through Dhiar's hair. "Sorry. I couldn't resist."

Dhiar only giggled and slipped away, leaping into the water and sliding through it like a dolphin, or any graceful creature of the sea. He breached the surface and leapt through the air, twisting a turn and diving again.

The angel could only watch with fascination, tucking his wings back and swimming much slower. Dhiar surfaced and flung powerful, loving arms around the other man, his Angel of Love, and kissed him again.

"Mmm... my element seems to be the water. Sometimes." The Incubus nipped at Siros's lower lip, then licked it. Below the surface of the water, he bumped his hips against the other man, growing more aroused with every second of contact. "Sometimes I feel like I could just curl up in a cave, or surround myself with fire, or melt into a tree... sometimes I feel like I ought to fly, just take to the sky... but I have no wings."

Siros gave back a series of tender kisses, never taking his eyes off Dhiar's. "Of course you do." He stretched out his own wings, sending water splashing around the two of them. "These are yours, to do with as you will."

Without another word, Dhiar let his hands slide down into the water, gripping at Siros's buttocks, each taking one and clutching. One hand slipped to the front and took both of their budding arousals, gliding up and down quickly, stroking them to fullness. He grinned and showed his sharp canines, sparkling in the sun. Even in a place like this, it still excited him to be doing something thought of as so naughty elsewhere.

"Shall we make the sea a little saltier?" The Incubus leaned in to kiss down the side of Siros's neck, to the top of his shoulder.

"Heavens yes," the angel groaned in return, already feeling as if he could not hold on a moment longer. Between the hours of temptation on the beach and the sensation of water surging around his loins, his body felt on the verge of bursting.

"Let's."

With that word alone, the pulses of pleasure crashed between them like the waves met the beach, and in that instant they merged again, their thoughts and feelings united by the pleasure and the senses.

28th Night
Oh To Be In Love

"I hope you're not getting bored with the Great City," Dhiar all but whispered, his arms coiled around the angel's as they continued down the path.

Siros looked suddenly to the side, to face the Incubus, smiling to him with a little surprise in his countenance. "How could I? It's endlessly interesting! There's countless places to go, countless things to do... and one magnificently special Incubus to do them with."

All around and above them curled the underground gardens, subterranean and lush below the city of Dis itself. The winding passages twisted this way and that, coming to entrances and exits like some sort of floral subway.

Vines and mosses grew over the walls of the corridors, strange bulbous flowers glowed in the low light, ice-chilled streams trickled down in little rock-cups to shimmering pools. In the air, all around, the water's pure, clean scent mingled with the scents of the soil, deep and rich and heady, and the rocks, the mosses, all of the life. Above it all, the delicate and subtle nectar of the aromatic dark-blooming flowers lingered at the nose. The place wove an elegant and elaborate tapestry for the senses.

Dhiar's cheeks coloured just a tad, and he rested his cheek on the angel's shoulder. "You always know what to say," he quietly murmured. "Even if it might be a little corny coming from anyone else."

"Oh, might it!" Siros chortled. Part of what drew him to Dhiar was his honesty, and indeed he had said demons had little occasion or need to lie, and he himself bore no talent for it.

Certainly, Dhiar could distract, and he could even make one forget, but to deceive was never a talent of his. Yet even when he was the most unapologetically honest he could be, something about his intrinsic charm made it impossible to hold it against him. The way he spoke, the way he phrased things... and those eyes, that smile... how could Siros bear a grudge?

He pulled the Incubus closer with a wing curled around him. "I think that's why you like me though, isn't it... admit it!"

"Of course it is." Dhiar turned to kiss the top of the other man's shoulder. "One of many, many reasons."

Each of the gardens had a different look to it. One would be short and small, another would open up to an expanse of greenery and little glowing spheres like firefly-light. Still another held a roaring underground waterfall, undoubtedly pouring from some place in the city. Another spread out like a terrace, with mosses like soft grass blanketing the rock underfoot, as if ready for a band of picnickers.

The two settled onto a vacant patch, holding onto each other. The moss was warmer than either had expected, especially with the variable warmth and chill of the gardens. Sometimes the darkness switched at seeming whim.

So many days they had whiled away in the Great City, in the Abyss. And yet here they found themselves, like so many days before their holiday, days spent in a subterranean city so very unlike this one. Dhiar placed his hand on Siros's chest and slowly rubbed in a widening circle.

"We'll have to get back soon, I think," he gently offered.

Siros nodded his head in return. "Yes..." Taking a deep breath, he let out a quiet sigh, but it echoed and lingered along the smooth stone around them. "We'll go back fresh, though. Fresh, refreshed, and stronger than ever from this."

"And we can come back anytime." Dhiar kissed from the corner of the angel's jaw to his chin, up to his lips, lingering for a moment and then nestling his nose back into his luxurious silken locks.

"It's funny that this makes me miss it. Noctemburg, I mean." Siros let his eyes wander along the dome-ceiling, along the vines and the clouds of green and luminescent white. "When we came here, I thought I'd never miss it again. But there's still plenty to do there, isn't there? And plenty we've not done. So many places we haven't been together. There's a restaurant I'd like to take you to, just outside of that place they call Angel Town..."

"Really?" Dhiar traced the outline of Siros's nipple, through his blouse. "Not stuck-up?"

The winged man grinned at the question. "Not at all! It's extraordinary."

The two shared another kiss. Dhiar slid his body halfway onto Siros's, covering him a bit like a living blanket. His warmth surrounded the angel. "Tell me about it."

"Well, it's a vegetarian place," Siros explained. "They have the best food... even a buffet at lunch and dinner that you can get. Really, you can get them to cook by request too, whatever you want! It's marvellous."

"I'm glad you remember that about me."

"What, the vegetarian thing...?"

"Mm hmm." Dhiar closed his eyes, squeezing Siros's far shoulder. "Some forget. It's not a huge thing, but for me... well, it's important. I can feel the past of items... things... and if something's in me and it isn't something that had a peaceful way of getting there..."

"It's unpleasant. Yes, I know. I care about that. And about you." Siros stroked his fingertips over the Incubus's cheek. "That's why I attend carefully to such things. I would never wish to bring you harm or discomfort. The time we have with each other should be the nectar of life."

A little smile spread across Dhiar's lips. "Oh yes. I like that. I like that phrasing. 'The nectar of life'... you're a poet, you know?"

"I fancy myself more of a dabbler," Siros replied, propping up one of his legs. "Not really anything serious."

"I don't mean... like writing them," Dhiar continued. "It's just the way you put things, you're so poetic. So artistic. Whatever your thoughts are, you always seem to... just make me marvel at the way you say them!"

"Let me make you marvel, then." Siros turned his head and leaned closer.

Dhiar took the hint and brought his lips to meet the angel's. And then he melted into them, mouth to mouth, warming in clouds of breath, in the gardens underground.

29th Night
Oh, Maker

Transitions were always the most exciting and dreadful parts of any journey. All the questions and possibilities presented hope and despair both, and none of them could be certain until the destination. As the old saying went, "getting there is half the fun".

This trip, however, ended quickly enough and the transition was brief indeed. Dhiar stretched as he lit a coal for the incense, placing it in the censer and hanging it from the hook he dedicated to it, in the shop. He brushed his hair back with his fingers, out of his eyes, and looked around.

Somehow, the shop floor seemed stark, and a bit uninviting. He would have to change that. The Incubus stalked into the storeroom and returned with some drapes and a footstool, reaching up and practically climbing about like a monkey to hang them. He hummed to himself as a soft drizzle began outside.

That was new, he reflected. Usually in Noctemburg, it either poured or the moisture congealed into a thick, soupy mist. To have a light, gentle rain must have meant something else changed while they were away. He smiled a little bit more to himself and continued with his task.

He hoped to have it all in place before Siros woke. Even if the trip back had been brief, scarcely the blink of an eye, saying farewell to one place and hello again to another caused stress to any traveller. Some transitioned through sleep, others through occupying their minds and dealing with it a little at a time. Siros and Dhiar, both ends of the spectrum, today occupied the building of Phantasies.

The Incubus finished with the last of the drapes, then looked to the storefront. "Now that... isn't quite right, either."

The fluorescence fit with Noctemburg, but it seemed so lurid after the subtle elegance of Dis. Dhiar quietly switched the window's lights off and set them aside, to be carefully wrapped and stored later.

The oriel window always looked beautiful, though. He couldn't change that much. That was his personal nook, his own personal zone if any place was in the shop. He had seen so much from that window. Much better than the broad, flat expanse of glass that had originally occupied its space.

An idea that had occurred to him a few days previous surfaced once more in his mind, and he returned to the storeroom. With a few minutes of paint, a saw, and some sandpaper, it was ready. He walked to the front of the shop and pulled it open, stepping out. With a little boost from the railing there, he hung the sign reading "Phantasies" on the wrought-iron post that curled like the smoke of the incense inside.

And the front door! He placed his hands on his hips, then brought one to rub his fingertips along his chin. That would not do; and so, from glass and metal came wood: heavy, sturdy wood, with a window at the top of it to show the sign reading "open" or "closed".

The Incubus returned inside and looked around. Yes, that was much better. The trip had changed plenty of things, and that suited him. That had been the whole purpose of the holiday. Perspective tended to be jarred and refreshed by a change of venue. Sometimes the only thing a creative endeavour needed was to be looked at from a different angle.

And of course, it felt good to return home. To be surrounded by the familiar things of his youth and nascent existence, and yet to see all the new and different, all of this felt like sweet, clear air after being shut in a stuffy closet. Here he was, back in that closet, in a sense.

His brow lowered. Did he really think of Noctemburg that poorly?

No, he decided, he did not. But the place had been his home for too long. Familiarity had bred contempt, as it sometimes tended to do. Not with Siros, of course. He could spend for ever with that angel...

Dhiar folded his arms over his chest and slumped back against the doorframe. Would Siros come with him? Where would he go in the first place, anyway? It troubled him. Could he even trouble the angel to follow him? He felt a distress and frustration that he so rarely allowed to alight upon his presence of mind.

But he would not allow it to reside there. It would not be like him, not like his personality or any part of him. He set it aside in his mind and took a deep breath of the sweetened, spiced air. He felt himself smile, and sigh, and then he slowly strode to the counter with the register.

Taking out a pad underneath, he produced a pen and began to tick off a few items he had noticed in his morning's work. Then, after a few minutes, he set the pen down and crouched behind the counter, fiddling with the things underneath and putting a pot on. Here he had secretly installed a pot and a little stove-eye for heat, just for making little things like tea without having to head upstairs and bring it down.

Dhiar pulled himself up and leaned back to lower himself into his chair. This chair always sat stacked high with blankets and cushions that the shape of the original piece of furniture had become indistinguishable and largely forgotten. But it was Dhiar's chair, his most comfortable seat. It seemed right, since he spent so much time there during any day.

The scent of steam mixed with the incense, and the Incubus got back to his feet and poured up the cup of hot water into the waiting teacup, with its silvery mesh ball of tea in it. Vanilla and rose, with a hint of cardamom. Could there be greater bliss? Dhiar thought not. The simple pleasures were, after all, often the most richly pleasing.

He watched the clear water turn dark, a mixture of red and black, like liquid garnets in the cup before him. His fingers curled around the curved body of the cup, and he brought it to his face.

It was good to be home, in Phantasies.

30th Night
The Last Day of Our Love

"You really have to go?" Dhiar pouted, sticking his lower lip out as his hands kneaded along the angel's foot. His thumbs circled outward, along the tissues and muscles and connections.

Siros looked down to the Incubus, slowly smiling, moving his toes. "Only for a little while," he murmured. "And I'm sure you won't be bored. There are plenty of handsome gentlemen in this city."

"And just handsome men who aren't so much gentlemen," Dhiar quipped, giggling as he worked his hands up over the angel's ankles, over his calves and shins, around his knees dallying and dipping his face down to kiss each once. "I'm sure there will be rapturous lovers where you'll be?"

"I doubt it." Siros laughed, lifting one leg slowly, rubbing the inner knee along Dhiar's shoulder. "I'll be back before you know it, and we'll pick right up. I'll miss you terribly... I'm so glad you understand."

Dhiar just laughed, nosing between the other man's legs, along his bare length. "I'm so glad you understand! It's so very rare to find a lover who can appreciate the differences... giving space, and giving respect and love."

"Respect and love are supremely important!" Siros chuckled, deep in his chest, the muscles tensing and his shoulders rolling back. He spread his thighs, the aroma of his arousal growing stronger as his shaft grew to stand, pointing to his stomach.

Dhiar moved carefully along the angel's erection, drawing his tongue up the underside and lapping at the tip. How he loved the feel of the supple flesh at his mouth! He could suckle at it, and it gave a bit. He slid his mouth down on it, then came back up again, smacking his lips and kissing the very end.

Siros let his eyes close, hand wandering through Dhiar's hair, his hematite curls. He would miss this so much. Even the slightest contact between them, the scantest touch, set his soul aflame. His heart thumped even seeing Dhiar's tongue slide between his lips to take a drink. His lips glistened pink and wet.

The slit dribbled clear, slick, sticky angelic precum. His head sparkled with it. The Incubus pressed his thumb to it and spread it around, watching the way it caught the light. He grinned again and dipped down, taking the length fully in his mouth. Sinking down, he nuzzled his nose into the fluffy patch of hair at the base.

The scent aroused him so much. Dhiar pushed his shorts down, wiggling his backside, bending knee and flicking the underpants off the bed. The Incubus sighed, stroking himself, already so hard, dripping, slick and wet and ready. He took in a slow breath through his nose, drawing up to the tip again, licking his lips.

"You can keep doing that as long as you like," Siros purred, shivering up his back and gripping at the back of Dhiar's head. "If you want, you can bring that happy little rod up here and I'll do my best to reciprocate."

Without a word in response, Dhiar turned his body, and then a sound issued forth from his throat as he felt the angel licking between his legs. He drew in a shaky breath, then returned to his work on his lover's pulsing, rigid cock. Reaching down, he pulled up at the balls, toying with them both and then each in turn, down underneath along to the circle of muscle marking his lover's entrance.

He had yet to have Siros in that way, though the night at the Pit had united them in the other. Dhiar grinned and then began to move quickly up and down, bobbing his head as he stroked his hand from the base, to meet his mouth. He could taste all of the excitement, and in anticipation he shivered again, eager. This was what he wanted. This would be a gift to remember.

Siros spread Dhiar's buttocks, kneading them, licking down on the Incubus's length and up to nuzzle his sac like a coin purse, a treasure velvety and secret. He would remember this. He could carry this with him, on his journey. And in the moment, he could love it, relish every moment as he did. Every touch, every caress, every taste and scent and the singular, unique visual perspective.

The heat between them rose, more intense with every passing second, each cycle down and then up again. Both men's skin tingled, both leaked incessantly, both made sounds mingling louder and louder as they neared the last crescendo. A few shallow breaths through the nostrils, and then both mouths were filled, muscles flexing, and Dhiar limply draped across Siros's body, legs spread in a v-shape at his head.

"Enough to remember?" The Incubus grinned over his shoulder, then turned back to kiss at the side of Siros's softening cock, still plump with the arousing nearness.

"I'll be counting the very seconds until I return. There will never be anything like this. Like you." Siros smacked his hand soundly against Dhiar's ample buttock, grinning down his body. "We are perfect for each other. I am more confident than ever it is so."

Dhiar curled his toes and let out a yelp at the swat. He rubbed his crotch against Siros's chest, settling down against him, skin to skin. "I thought so. From that first night..."

"In the garden."

"In the rain."

"Together with you."

Dhiar slowly coiled up, turning his body around to meet the angel's mouth with his own. "And we'll have that again, very soon."

"I promise. You have my oath, nothing will stop me from returning to you." Siros cupped the Incubus's cheek, looking longingly into his eyes. He kissed him again, breath hot and still smelling of Dhiar. "And you will be in my dreams and my heart."

"And you in mine." Dhiar kissed him again and again, over and over, as if he were trying to commit the taste and sensation to memory as vividly as possible. "So beautiful. So darling, so enchanting."

31st Night
Cherokee Louise

Miranda smiled a little, knowing smile, slight and mysterious, as she looked out the window. Dhiar sat across from her at the small table, back in his chair and watching her face.

Really, her golden hair, her fair features and rose-red lips, even without makeup—it was a feminine ideal. The parts that interested him the most were the little laugh lines on her face, the weathering that gave her such character at the corners of her eyes and her mouth. These things made her appear less of a doll and more of a real woman, whatever else her heritage contributed.

"I wonder sometimes if it's the place for me." The Incubus spoke, taking in a deep breath and letting out a sigh. "I wonder, too, if it's just the natural wanderlust of my kind, to see so many vistas, so many things... I've seen so much already, but I have an insatiable desire for still more."

Miranda's eyes only slowly returned to Dhiar, her smile widening to show her teeth. "If you feel the need to wander, wander."

"Is it that simple?"

"Hasn't it been?"

He tapped his fingernail against the wine glass, then brought it up to his lips. After taking his drink, he set it back down on the table. "I keep coming back."

"If you only come back out of obligation, when everyone else here has flown to the winds, that isn't what you really want. Is it?"

The silence passed between them. He glanced out the window. Lights sparkled like stars on artificial firmament made of buildings, buildings which stretched from the invisible street to the inscrutable sky.

"No," he answered at last. "No, you're entirely right. It isn't."

"It doesn't suit you to let yourself be miserable while you're waiting for something to happen so passively." Miranda lightly moved her glass in her hand, in a circle. The sweet red wine inside swayed and danced around. "You may be a prize like a princess in a storied tower, but you have the ability to leave that tower yourself."

And Dhiar knew she was right. That was why he had come to this bookshop again, to see her, to speak with her, to spend the quiet, cold night in pleasant company. But this quality was not limited to mere meaningless pleasantries; he wished to hear the truth.

"So," she continued, as he contemplated. "What about humanity?"

"What about them?" He answered, flashing a bright grin. It faded like embers after a cold night, his face gradually settling into a softer expression of contentment. Then it disappeared altogether, his thoughts turning again. "There are so many humans, so many kinds. Each one is different. Like any other type, I suppose. Species or race or what have you." He motioned with a hand, a flourish of the wrist. "It depends on the time, when you catch them. Sometimes they're marvellous as a whole, other times they're shameful."

Miranda laughed, a sound deeper and richer than her speaking voice. It was an old voice. It had quality to it, character that blithe, innocent voices missed in timbre.

"It's true!" Dhiar chuckled too, smacking his lips after another sip. "They tend to see time as linear, but it doesn't always lead to improvement. It's like a fine wine, sat to age in some cellar somewhere... but humans forget so easily, and so that wine might turn to vinegar before anyone recalls it."

She put a hand to her chest, calming and curling a bit in her chair. The seats were broad and winged, large enough to curl up in, for a nap. "It's different here."

"Humans don't steer the course of this city," Dhiar replied quickly. "It's more so-called creatures of the night. Humans are just a part of it."

"Some of them were humans once."

"They've lived so long that any with the power and influence have usually grown beyond it," he countered. "It's not like on the surface. On the surface, human society permeates. It's pervasive, it's everywhere. You can't avoid it. Even the vampires, as much as they would like to believe it's not a part of their existences anymore, there it is. They play and manipulate and all of it ends up being a puppet play on the same stage."

"Fear and shame govern widely."

"And regret. And anguish. I suppose it isn't a solely human quality, but people time travel throughout their lives. And they reincarnate even in the same existence." Dhiar leaned forward, propping his cheeks on his hands, his elbows on the table. "They float between a gilded past and a future of longing. The present doesn't tend to interest them much. It's hard to blame them."

"Hope must be preserved," Miranda noted. She breathed deeply in. The wine had started to make her stomach tingle. "Otherwise, why continue on another day?"

"And I suppose it all comes back around to the fact that most of them don't have the same mobility I do." Dhiar gave a little nod of his head, then sat upright again, resting his hands on the tabletop. "I could so easily pack up shop and make a place for myself somewhere else, somewhere there are no regrets every day, no thoughts and feelings that interfere with the breathing everywhere I look."

"You've become entangled in a place you never wanted, my friend." Miranda finished her glass and set it before her. "It's time to spread your wings."

"My proverbial wings," he corrected, with an impish grin.

She closed her eyes, smiling to his words.

Dhiar slipped up to his feet and walked to her side, taking her hand and kissing it. "Thank you, my friend. I hope we'll meet again very soon. And of course, you can come to Phantasies any time. I've left you with a card."

"Of course." Her eyes opened, radiant and jewel-like. She looked up to his. She wanted to remember him like this, lit by the cityscape behind him. "This is my home. My nest. But it's important for you to realise where yours is. You must fly for that to happen."

"I shall fly," he answered. "I shall soar!"

32nd Night
Wednesday

Of course, Dhiar thought to himself, this would have to happen when I was in the middle of packing.

He wasn't particularly worried, primarily because he had already set Phantasies on its way from Noctemburg; there would be no chance of anyone stumbling in and finding him gone, and no-one else to watch the shop. He would have to fix that, at some point. But then, he had never had this particular problem before, either.

He stood naked, skin tinged with reds and pinks, still fair enough to contrast his hematite locks that curled lightly about his shoulders. Apparently, his clothes were of the kind of material that did not weather whatever summoning this group had wrought.

All young, strapping men stood about him, congratulating each other, clasping hands, embracing in glee. Some wore more than others: most wore lengthy dark robes in crimsons and blacks, but it was easy enough to see through them the way they clung and draped over the smooth musculature of these slender lads.

The familiar smell of burning wicks met his nose, just as the sight of flickering, dancing candleflame met his vision. That seemed to explain it. He took a few steps to the redheaded, wild-looking man holding the thick book. A grimoire! Yes, he felt sure he knew what was happening here.

Dhiar swung his hips lightly, moving his broad shoulders, flexing his smooth chest. His curls bounced down, tumbling to his waist, just below which his length bounced too, from side to side. Its movements enticed the eyes, balls swinging heavy beneath. His eyes sparkled, gleaming deep and black in the darkness. He grinned, showing his bright teeth.

"Wait, er..." The redhead, who was clearly the ringleader of this little group, held up his hand to Dhiar. "You're... you're dismissed! We were just seeing if it worked...!"

"It doesn't work like that." Dhiar took the hand and pulled the lad to him, bringing lips to lips in a kiss so smouldering that one of the others fell to the floor in a faint.

The Incubus ran his hand down the front of the robes and rubbed where he knew he would find reaction. He drew his fingers to the tip of it, feeling the familiar give, the supple shape, under the too-thin cloth. That would have to go.

Quickly enough, it did. With a little help, the robe soon lay on the floor. All around, the other magicians looked on in a mixture of excited and bewildered, entirely unsure if they ought to lend some assistance or simply enjoy the show. Their summoned demon didn't seem to be violent or objectionable, just... eager. Eager to please.

And please he did, right to the hilt in the red ringleader's rear! The familiar slapping pleased him. He hadn't been like this lately. He hadn't been too much of a top, not particularly dominant or aggressive. It pleased him to assert that, to bring that back from where it slept in his breast. He reached down and touched the redhead once, on what the Incubus might playfully call his "magic wand," decorated by fiery red hair at the base. One touch was all it took.

Dhiar let himself release barely a moment after his new lover did. Pulling out while the younger man still felt little, in the throes of passion, he let him lean and slide his way down the wall, to sit.

The Incubus turned proudly to the others, beaming as he walked right out of the magical circle. It was silly, of course, but still charming and cute in its own way. He swept his arm before him in an arc.

"So! Who's next?"

Within seconds he was occupied at both ends, by a muscular and a little hairy lad at the mouth, a slighter blond behind him. Another blond, with nearly platinum hair, joined in around front, which made any movement whatsoever a shot of pleasure shared in a crashing wave, a burst, a ripple between all of them.

The intensity was too much for the hairy lad, though the blond lasted a fair bit longer. The platinum one, underneath, relished every taste of Dhiar's output: the precum tingled on his tongue and was powerfully sweet. When the blond buried in him once more and came in three huge bursts, Dhiar gave his own gift in turn to the one mouthing his own cock. It almost choked him.

Then the Incubus pulled away from the other boy, lying atop the platinum-haired lad and kissing him, tasting himself on the talented young man's tongue. Dhiar's penis began to fill, never having gone lower than half-mast; he ground his hips against the other man's, and his kisses deepened. His tongue teased, a little rougher than a human's, but then these magicians were not human themselves. Warlocks, Dhiar mused, judging by the ears and teeth and magical auras.

He hadn't had a Warlock in a while. It pleased him. He clasped both rigid rods in his skilled fingers, pressing them together side-by-side and pumping them at once. He could feel it building up in him again. His ass clenched, even though he was no longer occupied there, and the wave of bliss rolled over his body, between his loins and out, at just the same time his partner did the same. The lad called out, and his voice faded into incoherent moaning.

Another youthful Warlock, and another, and Dhiar's mind began to click to automatic pilot. He had the skill, the practice, the muscle memory... and what muscle! Each lay panting, catching his bearings, after a single tumble and roll. The juices of the body were plentiful, warm and sticky and wet and slick, fragrant and intoxicating. The perfumes mingled and filled the room, mixing the rich incense with the musky aroma of sex and youth.

Dhiar settled at last, getting his bearings, bringing himself to the here and now of the situation. He looked around himself and saw a room full of handsome young Warlocks with smiles on their faces, exhausted, sticky, sweaty and gorgeous. His eyes turned to his own body, gleaming, glistening, muscles shining and hair dotted with jewel-like beads of moisture. It made him laugh, and he stroked himself back to fullness.

"Who's for another round, lads? You'll never become archmagi by quitting so easily!"

A few lazy groans came in answer... but more laughter came, and with it crawling Warlocks with shining eyes.

33rd Night
Yuuwaku

Dhiar gazed out the oriel window. It no longer showed the street in Noctemburg that had become so familiar; now it looked out upon a swirling starfield, a vision beyond bounds of cosmos.

The shopkeeper smiled to himself, sitting down in the window with his cup of tea. The aromatic steam curled up around his face: rose, vanilla, and cardamom, with the rich and full body of black tea.

He decided the rest of his work could wait. They were nowhere he would need to open the shop yet, in any case. There would be no pressure to do so in the middle of the void. He had not hung between universes in so long... every time Phantasies had moved in the recent past, he could remember only jumping from place to place and back again. The brief jaunt to the Abyss had been so refreshing and yet so brief.

Perhaps he could go back there again. But he had only just been. That was no good. Above all, he didn't want to grow too used to the Great City, or ever to find it anything less than exciting. He could enjoy himself, certainly, but eventually he would be relegated to the same things as Noctemburg had crafted within him. Eventually it would bore him, and he found that possibility supremely distasteful.

He looked at the swirling thin foam atop his tea, light and vanishing into the black depths of the liquid. For an instant he found himself completely enthralled, and then he snapped his attention from it and looked out the window again.

Before his eyes spun the same vision, of lighter, brighter objects catching light and spinning like spirals around themselves in an endless cosmic dance.

"The universe, in a cup of tea." Dhiar smiled a little more, bringing the cup up to his lips and sipping from it.

It had become a favourite pastime of his, to blend teas and

place them in the thick glass jars on the shelf he made for them. They had earned their place in his shop and the esteem from his customers.

He would have to keep up with some of them. Most, he recalled, still had cards and could contact him if necessary. Lothring was one he would have to recall, with his regular visits. But existing outside of regular time made it easy to keep any appointment. Everything seemed to be in place. Miranda was correct. The time was right!

He lowered the cup between his hands, resting it between his palms. The shop had grown cold recently, even cooler than the regular weather in Noctemburg. It didn't offend Dhiar; it barely affected him. But he could feel it, and he liked to warm himself back up when he felt the chill around him. His body maintained a temperature higher than a human's. Absently he wondered if he should get some cats for the shop, since they always did like warm bodies and pleasant company.

Evvin's letter should arrive soon, Dhiar noted. Faithfully, the boy wrote him about his adventures with Anton. They travelled around Europe and then Asia, enjoying the best the lands could offer. Dhiar knew so many of the places he read about in the missives, although he visited them during different times. It saddened him, at least a little, to know that Evvin would likely never see them in their greatest glory.

Yet so much still existed, even in memory, and beauty and vitality persisted as if in spite of those who tried so hard to shut it up. He recalled the sensual temples and the Naga in the place now called India. His cheeks coloured and his smile turned to a grin. Quietly he chased it with another gulp of the rosy tea.

His chest spread, shoulders rising as he breathed slowly and deeply. That drink always calmed him so profoundly. Nothing else affected him so. Even chamomile left him merely coaxed into a slumbery state, but this tea, this one always made him comfortable and gave him sensual pleasures, weaving a complex temptation for his consciousness. Vanilla, rose, and cardamom provided a tantalising enough combination, but added to the backdrop of black tea made it completely undeniable, utterly unavoidable.

He breathed in the steam again, closing his eyes and letting his head fall back against the wall. Sleep would not come. He had no desire to slumber, or to dream, but to experience the images running through him and the sensations coursing through his body, it had to be concentrated upon with totality.

One hand slid down the soft skin of his chest, disturbing the laces crisscrossing over the open collar of his poet's shirt. It did not concern him in the slightest. He loved the feeling of skin to skin, and moreover the sense of fingertips on skin. Bumps rose like gooseflesh as he tickled the surface with the edges of his nails. His nipples firmed at the touch, and he idly swayed his fingertips between one and then the other.

His eyes suddenly opened. He knew what he had to do!

Swiftly he spun on his bottom and then unfolded, up to his feet. Setting the cup aside at the counter next to the register, he stepped behind it and began to rummage. This would not do! He knew exactly what was necessary. Exactly what was called for in this situation, he had to put hands on it.

At last, his fingers curled around it! It was his, it was his own, and he claimed it for himself. He stood again, holding it up to the light, unashamed—proud, even—at the sight, in the open. He licked his lips, shivering a little bit.

Yes, this would do nicely.

He couldn't stop giggling as he peeled the paper away from it, this lush dark chocolate bar, with honeyed rose petals in the chocolate, and a delicately-whipped nougat handmade. It was his favourite bar.

The cup returned to his hand, and he resumed his seat in the window, sipping and nibbling in turns. Yes, he thought, that was how to do it!

34th Night
Romance Way

Who could resist the siren-call of Dhiar's appearance? Even those not swayed by his visual impact would surely be won by his sweet tones and well-chosen words, or his touch, his delicate strength, the way he moved, swaying his hips just enough to bring attention to them.

His black curls, raven as the night and waving into ringlets in front of his hidden ears, the little twin horns that barely showed in his sea of hair, and his angled brows; his deep, dark eyes like the red dahlia clothed in shadow, his noble nose, his lush lips—these all took the vision and made it theirs. His neck continued long and slender, the angles leading to his broad shoulders and curved chest. His waist came in slender, but not too slim, his thighs powerful and continuing the arc of his buttocks, calves just rounded and feet the graceful feet of a dancer or perhaps an acrobat. The aspect which made his masculinity clear always arranged itself in just the perfect way in front, filling any trousers that could be made to fill and moving with exactly the right amount of suggestiveness with others that hung too loose and open.

He pursed his lips as he tossed off another waistcoat. "That won't do at all!"

With a sigh, he drew another onto his arms and pulled it on the rest of the way, over his loose-fitting white poet's shirt. The front dipped down to show his chest's centre, bare to midriff, and he smiled at the sight in the mirror, arranging the laces just so.

"Yes," he said to himself, "I think that'll be fine."

The trousers he wore were different than he had worn before: these were made of an almost velveteen material, deep red to match the waistcoat and his eyes and laced at the hips instead of fastened at the front. Tantalising glimpses of bare skin were afforded by the woven laces hanging tied at his waist.

He pulled on boots, a sublime and easy cuff at his calves, with the faintest embroidery. He looked, in a word, like a prince or some well-to-do noble. Appropriate, he thought as he glimpsed himself in the mirror, as he was a prince technically, with the mother of all his kind their queen.

Once satisfied, he set himself to cleaning up the clothes strewn around him for his little fashion show. A new place, a new wardrobe! It made sense to him.

A second before the door opened and disturbed the chimes next to it, Dhiar already looked in that direction. When the visitor entered, he raised a hand and his voice in greeting.

"Welcome to Phantasies!" The clothes quickly were put aside, to tend to later, and he made his way to the front.

There stood a young man, handsome and strong, but still bearing the slightest rounded cheeks and youthful glow. His eyes were older than his age, and his mien direr than his appearance. Barely clad in anything, the tunic he wore didn't quite cover below his waist when he moved. He swung free, and buttocks bounced pert and well-honed. Dhiar could tell he was very muscular under the threadbare material.

"Er... sorry, I just..." The young man glanced back out the window, not wanting to meet Dhiar's gaze. "I thought I might rest in here a moment. It's warm..."

"Why not come with me!" Dhiar reached out and took the lad's hands, drawing him farther into the main store. "Let's have a bath, and a meal. Which would you have first?"

Something was different about his guest. He couldn't put his finger right on it, but he knew there was something non-human about him. Still, he figured it couldn't be his business until he was informed. The younger man seemed too stunned to answer.

"I am Dhiar. This is my shop! And I live here. What are you called?"

"Joshua," the other man looked into those eyes for the first time, and it was as if electricity pulsed between their woven fingers. "I... uh, I shouldn't trouble you." But his tone made it clear that he didn't want to be made to go.

Dhiar just grinned, his toothy, wide grin that shone stellar. "It's no trouble, of course!"

Without hesitation, he reached over and let Joshua's hands fall to his sides. With barely even a token effort, the tunic was removed and tossed aside. And then, continuing on without a word, he easily and quickly removed his own clothes, the ones he had spent some time carefully selecting, and he stood naked before his new friend.

"There! Nothing to be ashamed of. Come." Again the Incubus took Joshua's hand and led him behind the silk dressing screen which hid the door to the stairwell up. He glided gracefully up to the door of the loft and inside.

Joshua caught his breath as he walked in. It wasn't a huge place, no palace or château, but it projected a homeliness and welcome that he had only rarely experienced before. It was warm, in every sense of the word.

"Do you like it?" Dhiar bounced, hand in hand.

Joshua's eyes were drawn south, to see what bounced so much more excitedly than the man himself. "Yes... yes I do!" Hurriedly, cheeks pink, he looked back to Dhiar's face.

But the Incubus only seemed to find it amusing, and he led through a lush red bedroom to a bathroom. Flowering, live plants sat around in pleasure of the regular steam and moisture, a garden tub sitting under a skylight.

Dhiar walked to the tub and started the water, releasing his guest and stepping into the tub. He lowered himself, draping his body along the side facing out, legs spread without a hint of shame. His hair dallied in the collecting water and began to swirl on the rushing ripples.

"Choose our bath salts and join me," he coaxed. "I'm partial to vanilla, and rose."

Joshua at last smiled. He had some sharper teeth than Dhiar, and with his bushy hair moving this way and that, the Incubus noticed a peculiar fur in his angled ears. He certainly wasn't human! But Dhiar looked forward to learning his true nature... later.

Now was the time for welcoming.

35th Night
Say You'll Go

Dhiar sat sipping tea in the oriel window, reflecting on the recent past. The months previous had been spent far away from Noctemburg, with a contemplative solitude for part. A letter from Dhiar's sister changed all that.

"Little brother, you have to come and spend some time here! It's the berries!"

As usual, he did not quite understand the entirety of what she meant by what she said. Her words were always chosen from the vernacular speech of her favourite period, the 1920s. And in the endless layers of dimensions and worlds in the cosmos, stacked like onion-skin infinitely, there was one such place where the period lasted indefinitely. It was a time of excitement and what Chana gleefully called "new thrills".

When Dhiar arrived, he shut Phantasies up and flipped the sign to read "closed" to the outside world. The shop always seemed to take the place of vacant buildings, just for the time it was there; passers-by would just think it was closed whenever they passed. What an odd store, they might think. It never seems open.

He almost stepped out in his usual attire, but after a little consideration he changed his mind: instead, he wore a suit more appropriate to the time, with braces and even a happy little hat made of straw and ribbon.

The speak-easy made his head swim with the different smokes mingling, the people packed into such a small area, and the music drowning out the rest of the attempts at conversation. He spotted Chana immediately, but without saying anything, she led him back past a strong-looking man at a door and into another lounge entirely.

Here the place was quieter, with intimate conversations between the pleasant people, and all sipping a variety of drinks. Alcoholic drinks, Dhiar could tell.

One of the disadvantages of the period was the ridiculousness of

Prohibition, making alcohol technically illegal; the speak-easy proved it was not particularly difficult to get, nonetheless. Chana brought two cocktails to their table and set them down, one on each side, and sat with hers, motioning for Dhiar to take the seat in front of his.

She clasped his hands excitedly, before he had the chance to take a sip of his drink. "Oh little brother, I'm so glad you came! You'll see. This is going to be just what the doctor ordered!"

He couldn't help himself, and he smiled at her enthusiasm, squeezing his fingers around hers. "I'm glad for the company."

The thoughts and feelings running through his mind since leaving Noctemburg had left him despondent and disillusioned, but he knew somewhere in his heart that it was only because it felt like he had failed, somehow. He hadn't. He had just outgrown the place. It no longer suited him or his life, his choices, or the things he wanted.

How often, he mused to himself, does one stay in a place only because it has been home for so long? At the point it ceases to be home, why is it not left behind? A variety of reasons, none of which he could say applied to him. He could pick up and leave at any time. Just as his friends in Noctemburg had mostly done as well.

The singer in the lounge had such a different sound than the one outside, probably by design: the one inside, in the secret room, crafted her art with a silken-smooth voice that coaxed at the ears and soothed the soul, even while breaking the heart with the words she sang. Dhiar took in a deep breath and slipped his hands back, to take up his glass with one and raise it in salute to Chana.

"What shall we toast to? We're supposed to toast, aren't we?"

She grinned, raising her own glass in response. "You're right! What should we toast to... I don't know, I hear 'to absent friends' all the time."

"To absent friends, then." Dhiar's eyes darkened slightly, his smile faded only a little, but it returned better and brighter than before as he lifted his glass to touch it against his sister's, then brought it to his lips, to drink.

"To absent friends," she echoed.

They drank quietly for a time. Both looked a million miles away at one instant, completely and utterly there the next. They could do that so well, much better than most of the humans around them. The others in the lounge probably had not the slightest clue as to the nature of the two at that table.

"You look good," Dhiar spoke at last.

"Thanks!" And Chana did, of course: from her deep scarlet flapper dress, a flat rectangular block with a little frill, to her gumdrop-shaped hat, her insouciant hairstyle, her polished-to-shine shoes, she cut a striking image. "You look pretty grand yourself. Where'd you scare up that outfit?"

"Scare... oh!" Dhiar chuckled, looking down at himself. "Well, I am a tailor. I just modified a few things. The hat was in storage somewhere. You know I've got all those storage spaces in the shop."

She smiled again, motioning with the hand holding her drink. "I still have yet to see this lovely shop! I've heard about it from Lydia and Lydie."

The memory of the twins' visit brought a smile to Dhiar's face now. "Yes... they seemed to like it quite a lot..."

"They did! They couldn't stop talking about it." She laughed now, setting her glass down after another sip. "Want to go back there and have some coffee or something? We can go from there to the party later."

"Party?" Dhiar's brows shot up.

"You didn't think I was going to have you come to see me and not show you a good time, did you?"

"I suppose not." He turned his glass around slowly, by the lip. "Are you sure it's something where I'll be welcome? I don't want to bring your night down."

"Please." Her response was dry and dismissive. "Like you could bring it down! Anyway, these parties are dime-a-dozen. I don't know a night where there's not a party going on. You should just let go of all those sob sister feelings and cut loose for a few hours. You're sure to get a few bites!"

"Bites, eh?"

"Interest." Chana gestured vaguely. "You know."

"I think I'm going to be very interested in this party." Dhiar grinned broadly.

36th Night
Gimme Sympathy

The party disappointed Dhiar. Chana lost herself in the crowd, leaving the Incubus floating free and quite overwhelmed by the miasma of conflicting feelings in this group. Anxiety seemed the most prominent feeling in the place, fear, confusion, loss, nervous desire... there was very little of the pleasure that made up the stuff of his existence. It frustrated him.

As he turned to the doors that led out to the garden, he nearly collided with a man, somewhere in his early twenties surely; he had the glow of youth with only a slight tempering of maturity. Mainly it was in his eyes, with a depth that even the oldest in this salon did not share.

"Terribly sorry!" Dhiar held up his hands cheerfully. "Just needed a breath of air."

"Air's a valuable commodity. Come on." The other man reached out to take Dhiar's hand, leading him out with a tentative grin.

It felt so much lighter outside, a definite relief. Though the town-house where the party was held had only a small garden, it was enough of one to provide something of an escape from the stifling heat and emotional density indoors.

"I'm Merry."

"You look it!" Dhiar beamed at his new friend. "I am Dhiar." With a slight bow at the waist, he lifted the man's hand and kissed it. "And flirty, of course."

Merry was struck speechless for just a moment, then he laughed, cheeks a little pinker than before, eyes gleaming as they reflected the soft lamp-lights from the windows. "You're a different sort of fellow than they usually have at their parties. I don't think I've seen you before."

"You haven't!" The Incubus spotted a little bench, made of wrought iron and wood, and led Merry by the hand to it, offering for him to sit first. "My sister took me along. I've just arrived in town, so she thought it might be something to get my mind off of... well, just a little melancholy really. It's nothing too crucial."

"But it still concerns you, right?" The other man sat, keeping his hand in Dhiar's as the Incubus joined him.

"Yes." Dhiar nodded a single time, leaning forward, gesturing with his free hand, fingers flowing in motion with strange grace. "I feel like... I don't know. I needed a change of venue. And now I need a change of venue from a change of venue so I can forget about the change of venue." He started to laugh.

Merry reached up, finally taking his hand back, and clapped Dhiar's shoulder. "This is a pretty fair party, for these parts. But you looked like you were looking right through everyone."

Dhiar wanted to say he had, but the explanation would have been too much for him. He didn't want to go into it. Not there or then.

"I'm a keen judge of character."

"You look it."

A few more moments of quiet passed between them. Then, slowly, Merry leaned against Dhiar's shoulder, resting his cheek against it and closing his eyes.

Dhiar turned his head, a little grin playing at the corners of his mouth. The man had a sweet scent, a pleasant scent. He had obviously slapped on some orange blossom water as his eau de toilette. It pleased the senses without being overwhelming or outright unpleasant, like some of the ambergris perfumes. There was a scent of some sort of styling medium in his hair, but it too remained light and inobtrusive.

And there, behind it all, was the scent of his body, of his skin, and it was clean and wonderful and mingled with the clothes he wore. Dhiar leaned closer, arranging his body just a bit, before leaning his head against Merry's.

"It's comfortable being with another fellow," Merry at last spoke, breaking the silence between them. "It's why I came to the city."

Although it wasn't really what Dhiar thought of as a city, not after Noctemburg. The place where he had met his sister definitely classified as one, but it was a smaller city, with a large amount of what would later probably become suburbs. It wasn't so built up. There was a smallish area of downtown business and bustle, but it was also easy to escape that and come to more residential places. The countryside lay within barely minutes by car.

Dhiar reached his hand to Merry's short hair and stroked through it, producing a happy little sound from the man. "So you came to the city to be with fellows?"

"Yes... you can keep doing that as long as you like," Merry answered quickly. "Yes, it's better than a little farming town. Sometimes I miss my family, but... I don't think they'd have understood, anyway. It's nicer here. More to do."

"More fellows to be with!" Dhiar chuckled, lightly tracing his fingertips down the man's cheek, over the line of his jaw. He noticed very well that a little bit of a curve remained of youth, and the jawline was not yet as strong as it would surely one day be. He could envision what his new friend would look like in only five or ten years: at his prime, a breathtaking example of manhood.

But now he was no slouch either. The Incubus found himself charmed by the earnest gentleness and uncertainty shining in Merry's gaze. The man looked to him, unsure, and then he laughed, knowing he wasn't being ridiculed.

Dhiar took his hand and raised it to his own cheek, pressing the fingers to his face. "You can touch me, you know. I don't mind. Just between us..." he leaned closer, quieting his voice, "I'm here to be with fellows too."

Merry's face went red, his heart pounding in his throat. He leaned closer, keeping his hand on the other man's cheek. His eyes closed and, almost trembling, he leaned up, up, just before Dhiar's lips.

The Incubus pressed in for a perfectly chaste kiss. But, being exactly who and what he was, that was enough for Merry's eyes to open wide.

37th Night
Night Scented Stock

Dhiar felt Merry. More specifically, he felt the man's body against his own, and it made him happy. He had said farewell to Chana at the party, expressed that he would see her the next day sometime, and then they returned to Merry's flat.

It was hardly a glorious or luxurious residence, but it was nice and warm and intimate, and as it was on the edge of the city, it was more generous than inner-city life would have given. Presumably, it was also less expensive. Dhiar always reflected on the strange dynamic of human value, especially in cities. On one hand, some of the places were very close to trendy spots, and on the other, they were often tiny, squalid little affairs. Other places weren't so convenient to trends, but they were much more pleasant to live in; yet somehow they often seemed the cheaper of the two options.

For whatever reason, Merry had chosen where he lived, and so there they were. It was a very small building, probably only five tenants at most. And that included the landlord, who from Merry's telling was a small old man who endlessly lamented the Gay Nineties.

Oh, what Dhiar could say to that!

"Would you like something to drink? I've some cordials, and a little bit of wine... there's water, of course, but it's a little hard."

"It happens to the best of us!" Dhiar cheerfully answered. "I'd like to share a cordial, I think. Could we?"

"Share... in the same...?" Merry turned to face the wall, digging in the tiny little cabinet barely occupied by a scant couple of bottles.

Dhiar gave a single nod, arranging himself on the little seat. It seemed to be a sort of couch, but it would more closely be termed a love sofa simply because of its small size. There was a mismatched chair, and then a divan that looked like it had survived the Victorian period, but it remained in good enough condition. Still, of all the choices, this was Dhiar's favourite. He crossed his legs at the knee, one atop the other, and bounced his foot.

"Please!" He at last called out, looking around the place and having noticed that Merry was looking the other way.

It always interested Dhiar to feel the places that he visited. At home, in Phantasies, the temperature was always perfect, always just right: that slightly cool temperature, but not so much that it made one shiver or feel like putting on more clothes. It was just enough to be comfortable. But this was a period, Dhiar remembered, long before widespread air conditioning and central temperature control in most of human civilisation. He noted the little slits of open windows, to keep air circulating, and the slight staleness of the room due to it having been shut up for the past few hours.

It was warmer than he usually found ideal, but all the same it didn't unsettle him. What he loved most about a warm room was the increased temperature of its inhabitants.

As Merry walked over with the single little glass, a crystalline thing that looked like a personal treasure, he chanced an unsteady smile. Dhiar breathed in, and he could smell not only the familiar scent of Merry, but also the less familiar scents of his body warming, a little sweat, and a little bit of the scent held by his furniture, and his bed... the scents that mingled and gave such a gentle indication of what the foundation of the scent of this man was.

"I've... never actually had a drink out of the same glass before..." Merry sat stiffly next to Dhiar, turning to look in his eyes.

The Incubus reached over and brushed the stray hairs from the younger man's forehead, smile radiant and reflected in his eyes. "Don't worry! I don't have a cold or anything."

He reached out and raised not the glass alone, but the glass in Merry's hand, and sipped gingerly, licking his lips, which gleamed with sweetness afterwards. Then Merry tentatively took a little bit of the drink himself, lowering the glass.

He averted his eyes for an instant, and then there was Dhiar, right at his face. He couldn't say anything, mouth full of cordial, sweet and lingering. It was difficult to swallow suddenly.

And then Dhiar's mouth was on his own, and he parted his lips to accept him. The tastes of cordial and the tastes of both men mingled, and it tingled through both of their bodies like electricity, the same electricity reflected by the primitive wiring that hummed in the walls, that flickered the stark bulbs giving the room some scant illumination.

It felt like forever before their lips separated. It felt like forever, but in reality only half a minute had passed, and barely that. Merry looked up at Dhiar and grinned sheepishly, cheeks burning red.

"Oh, don't be so bashful!" Dhiar laughed, tickling under the man's chin. "Oh... what's wrong? Did I do something wrong?"

"No, I... I..." Merry looked away and handed off the cordial to Dhiar. "Excuse me... for a moment. I need to... freshen... myself, just a little bit."

Then he rushed off. Dhiar had felt a little spark, a little—no! His eyes widened as he noticed it, and his grin spread. He had made the man climax just with a kiss! Just that! And as much as he enjoyed it, he hadn't noticed quite as much as he should have. Perhaps it was the cordial. Perhaps it was the company. Usually the inexperienced gave the most powerful, and the most authentic, honest of pleasure of that kind.

Dhiar started to undo his shirt and moved to the divan with his little glass, carefully. By the time Merry returned, dressed in a different pair of slacks, Dhiar had undressed to his trousers and arranged himself like a cloth across the divan, as if he himself were made of silk.

"Welcome back!" He called out to the man, raising his glass. "How are you for sip two?"

38th Night
Many Moons

They hadn't done anything particularly naughty. But it was shortly after the cordial had been finished, and both Dhiar and Merry were naked and laughing. They lounged in the tub, filled with warm water. It started out hot, but it had cooled. With the both of them in it and the room so warm, it stayed at a comfortable temperature.

Dhiar splashed a bit at Merry, who shielded his face and then splashed back.

"I've never really done this sort of thing!" Merry offered again, as if to justify it all. "My baths have always been strictly solitary affairs."

Dhiar's grin curled upward. "Baths are so much more fun when they're group efforts! At least pairs." He wiggled his toes and nudged at Merry's side with his foot. "Being naked doesn't have to be sexual. But it's always sensual."

The spot Dhiar touched was a ticklish one. Merry squirmed and giggled, blushing at the sound that came from him. He couldn't curl up or turn away with the way they sat, one at each end of the tub, legs spread around the other's.

The Incubus knew it. He had the other man in a position he could not easily extract himself from, and with a smooth motion, he moved his foot from the side of the chest, near the armpit, over the nipple, along the chest, then down the stomach. Carefully he stroked his toes over the man's navel, and then below... and the water sloshed around him.

Merry had been unable to calm himself, at least certain parts of himself, since he found himself naked with Dhiar. And though he wasn't overly large in that portion of anatomy, Dhiar liked the shape and size; it wasn't too much in either direction, maybe a little smaller than most, but it had a nice angle and curve to it. He glided his toes over it and pressed against the man's body, pushing the skin up along it and then pulling it down again, grinning widely at him.

Merry at last breathed in and closed his eyes, letting his head rest against the light blue tiles behind it. He spread his arms along the tub's curve, moving his hips a little bit. No protest came from him. Dhiar could feel his pleasure, welling up and brimming to the top. This man had not been touched many times, possibly never in the spot the Incubus now stroked with his foot.

Dhiar lifted his balls under the water, propping them on his toes and then letting them drift down. Then he slipped the erection between his first toe and second, stroking faster. He remembered, some time ago, how he had worked on his technique with his feet. There was a man like a monkey who seemed to be as good with his toes as he was with his fingers; Dhiar, naturally, had to learn his secrets.

He liked it when people, instead of fighting physically, had contests of stamina instead. Especially when he could decide exactly which event determined that stamina.

Merry swallowed hard. He almost couldn't stand it. Dhiar was holding back more than he usually did, knowing the other man's inexperience. Little ripples of pleasure emanated from him, as if they travelled on the water between them, mingling and surrounding them in gentle heat. The water was growing hotter.

Dhiar played with his friend, and poor Merry could hardly make a move. But the Incubus required no reciprocation. The pleasure of his partner was the most important. With that, he could get not only his own happiness, but sustenance as well. Such inexperience gave the most intense and satisfying food, of sorts. He relished the taste resonant through his body, that of intense, unbridled pleasure, thrill to the core of one's being, uncertainty, nervousness, all combined in a delectable dish breathing into the Incubus's body like perfumed mist. And it was perfumed with the scent of arousal.

Dhiar's leg moved gracefully up and back, revealing more about his own body. It was easy to see as his cock, half-erect but not really stiff, rolled along his body, his sac like a coin purse leaning to the side, slack and tender in the heat, the hairs along his crotch swaying in the water all around. The pink ring of his entrance showed itself every time he moved just so.

As Merry opened his eyes, looking down, half forcing himself to do it, he could see glimpses of it. It fascinated him, his eyes widening, his mouth hanging open, lips just parted. He suddenly breathed in a sharp breath and sighed it shakily out. Suddenly white wisps spread in the water along his stomach. Dhiar echoed the sound, deep in his chest.

"Mmm..."

The only sound between them for at least five minutes was that of water lightly sloshing. At last, Merry turned his eyes to Dhiar's face, looking at the Incubus and all of his features, so placid and relaxed.

"Dhiar?"

"Yes, my dear?"

"Was that... that was okay, right? That was all right?"

"That was lovely." Dhiar winked and blew a kiss, delicately rubbing the side of his foot against Merry's ribs.

"I've..."

"Never done that kind of thing before, I'm guessing?" The Incubus leaned forward, reaching to place his hand squarely on Merry's chest. "It's all right. You shouldn't feel anything but good about it. It felt good, didn't it?"

"Yes. Yes, of course it did, but..."

"No buts. It felt good. It didn't hurt anyone. On the contrary, it helped me." Dhiar leaned closer.

Merry leaned in to meet him, and the two's lips met.

"You're so mysterious, Dhiar. You're so... so... you're like the sheik and I'm just this clueless virgin swept into your world."

"I'm a sheik!" Dhiar chuckled, tickling under Merry's chin. "I'm like Valentino, am I?"

"Definitely better." Merry ran his fingers over the centre of Dhiar's chest. "At least, in my opinion. If I may buck popular opinion. I think you're far more handsome. But then, I can look right into your eyes. I can see you right here in front of me, in all your rich colours."

Dhiar kissed again, rising a bit and moving to lie half-atop Merry, so that they could coil at the same end of the tub. "And you, and all your rich colours. Seen and unseen."

39th Night
Down to You

Despite wishes to the contrary, Dhiar and Merry could not neglect everything else to spend all their time together; Dhiar had Chana to placate, and Merry his own work to do and things that demanded his time. So the day found the Incubus in town with his sister, strolling down a street filled with life.

Racks of clothes sat outside some of the shops, coaxing passers-by, while just a short distance away, people sat on the terrace to sip their teas and coffees in the clear weather. A familiar breeze rustled Dhiar's curls.

"We'll have rain."

"What, really?" Chana stopped at her brother's pronouncement and looked up to the sky, shielding her eyes with her hand. "Looks so clear."

"Trust me." He grinned to her, sliding an arm around her waist. "Let's go in here. You can feel it coming."

His mind drifted among the fine clothes, all made so well. He could have some of them in his shop, if he wanted. Still, he preferred all handmade. He ran his fingers along the sleeve of a shirt. They were priced low, especially considering the difference in time. No wonder Chana liked it here.

"What do you think of this?" Chana held up a shirt, ostensibly a man's shirt, but it seemed to suit her.

Dhiar nodded his head. "You should try it on! I think it might go well with some knickerbockers."

Her eyes lit up. "Ooh!" And so at once she tore off into the maze of shelves and racks, in search of her quarry.

He moved more slowly into the place, greeted by a worker or two and rummaging through the garments offered. Few things leapt out at him, but he liked the styles enough to keep going. A green blouse here and a pair of crimson trousers there finally took his fascination, and he went to try them on in the little rooms provided.

They were clearly not meant to go together, but they fit well and didn't seem to clash much. He could probably pull it off, if he wanted to wear them at the same time. But he had other clothes that he knew they would suit much better. As he pulled them off and replaced them on the hangers, his mind raced with the different ensembles. He pulled his own clothes back on again.

"How about it?" Chana stood just outside the curtain in her new outfit, men's shirt and knickerbockers. "Ain't it an eyeful!"

Dhiar couldn't help laughing, nodding his head. "I like it. You should get it."

"What d'you have there? Found something too?"

"Yes, I thought—" But he trailed off as the sudden roar of rainfall outside met his ears. He looked out through the front window, where the shopkeepers scrambled to pull the racks safely under the eaves, free from splashing.

"You were right!" Chana clicked her tongue, out of disbelief more than spite. "I don't know, that's beyond me. Looks like we're in for a rainy afternoon."

Dhiar took a deep breath in and sighed it out. His smile remained, and he began to walk back to the sales floor with all its racks.

"We'll have a rainy evening, but that shouldn't stop us." He knew it wouldn't stand a chance of stopping Chana. She would have her fun, rain or shine.

She slipped back into her changing room and quickly replaced the new outfit with the dress she had worn in, rectangular and straight, barely a curve in its design. She returned the cloche to her head, making sure her light curls were just so, and joined her brother outside.

"So were you thinking about a show? Maybe cabaret?" She went ahead to the sales counter, to leave her chosen garments and Dhiar's, then returned to him again. "You know, you really should let me take you to Berlin. I have a feeling you'd never want to leave."

Dhiar reached out and pulled a shirt off the rack, holding it first up to himself, then out towards Chana, tilting his head to the side.

He closed one eye, appraising, and then opened it again and returned the garment to its previous place.

"Sometimes blue looks good on me." She flashed a smile, throwing her head back and then laughing, airy, blissful and free.

"I'm more a fan of red. Nice cut though." He worked his way through the rest of the clothes. "What's in Berlin?"

"Oh, *everything!*" Chana bounced in place, her heels clicking on the floor. "There's cabarets and clubs and bars and dance halls, and of course Germans—" a melodious titter drifted between her lips, "and of course there's all kinds of new and exciting dance. Anita Berber!" She reached out to clasp at his shirt-sleeve. "We must see Anita Berber! Oh, it'll be such darb!"

It took Dhiar a moment. "If it makes you happy," he murmured, turning and leaning back against the hanging blouses behind him. "I'm just as content here, where we are."

"The continent is always more enlightened." Chana tickled her finger under his chin. "Ready to blow?"

He raised an eyebrow.

"Ready to *leave*," she clarified quickly.

"Ah! Yes!"

She rolled her eyes, still grinning, leading to the register and opening her purse. Before Dhiar could do it, she paid for all of the clothes and hefted both bags into her hand.

"I like the look of having a lot of packages," Chana explained, as they walked out under the eaves again. The rain had slackened a bit, but it still came down heavily. The former crowd of coffee-drinkers on the terrace had migrated inside.

Dhiar laughed as the two of them practically danced to stay under the eaves, under the shield of fabric and canvas and metal, and at last they ducked into the cafe. It was warm inside, warm and fragrant, with the scent of mingling teas and coffees heady on the air. Conversation surrounded them, bright eyes and bright faces.

"So what are you having?" Chana strode over to the counter.

Dhiar followed close behind. "What are you having?"

Chana smirked, rouged lips glistening. "We'll have two Turkish style."

40th Night
Scenery

Another night passed in a smoky club. All of Chana's favourite clubs were underground, figuratively if not literally; every last one of them required some sort of secret to access, which heightened the appeal for the Succubus. To her, predictability and ease chipped off great chunks of anything's allure.

In Dhiar existed a similar sort of sentiment, although it became somewhat daunting that literally every place they went required some considerable procedure only to walk through the door. It exhausted one before even procuring a table.

The performance bolstered his energy, however. The jazz number on-stage ended, the smoky-voiced singer walking to the bar to get himself some refreshment. Dhiar had to admit, there was an appeal to the smart dressing and slick hair, a handsome look out of a men's clothing advertisement. The clothing this man wore was a bit too crumpled and tired to be anything new, but for a soulful singer it worked well.

The Incubus made his way over. Chana was busy anyway on the other side of the room, hobnobbing with casual acquaintances who would never dream of refusing conversation with her.

"That was magnificent," Dhiar called out to the other man. "Let me buy you a drink."

"Just water, if you please." The singer answered with an appreciative nod and a smile. His features were dark, his skin tanned, and there existed a kind of exotic quality to his face. "I appreciate the praise. Usually I'm not much more than a decoration to go with people's enjoyment of illicit drinks."

Dhiar signalled the bartender, who quickly moved to provide two glasses of water. The Incubus presented one and held the other up, saluting as in preparation for a toast.

After half the drink had been drained, well within a minute's time, the singer returned his eyes to the man before him. "I'm Tommy. Well," he caught himself, "really that's my stage name. Everyone calls me Tommy. It's Tomas, or it was."

"Tomas. I like that." Dhiar motioned to his own chest with his free hand. "I am Dhiar."

"Dhiar!" Tomas repeated, sounding out the zh syllable first. "That sounds exotic! I take it you're not from around here? Or did you just come to the city?"

"My sister invited me." He motioned across the room. It was impossible to miss Chana, as usual. The huge red-tinted pheasant feather in her headdress flagged her easily above the rest of the crowd. "I've just been taking some time away. I've just moved from a place I spent a lot of time in, so now I'm wanting to... just sort of..." He motioned vaguely. "Not forget it, but distract myself."

Tomas set his now-empty glass down and clapped Dhiar's shoulder. "Well, if you'd like to distract yourself after the set, I'm going to the Turkish baths down the street." His eyes glimmered, like tumbled black stones. "I'm told my mother was Turkish. Just keeping it in the family."

With laughter, they parted at that moment.

An hour and a half later, surrounded by steam and naked otherwise, the two sat in a large domed room. Muscles glistened and moisture beaded on supple skin, giving it almost the appearance of candied fruit.

Tomas had a nice body, Dhiar reflected. Not too thin, shoulders just broad enough, and perky between the legs, though somewhat relaxed by the heat. He made no attempt to disguise his wandering eyes, and Tomas certainly didn't seem to mind, leaning back and spreading legs and arms, as if coincidentally.

"It's busier here earlier in the morning and later at night. This is always the best time to come with friends." Tomas stretched his arms up and moved to the side, draping himself over Dhiar's lap and grinning up at him. "Or the best time to come if you want some privacy."

"You'd better watch it, that can be dangerous territory!" Dhiar laughed, reaching down to walk his fingers through Tomas's chest hair, stretching out like a bloom from the centre of his chest. "Sometimes spikes come up and poke at the back of your head."

The singer wiggled his head, chuckling and folding his hands over his stomach. "I'll just have to take that risk! So... tell me a bit more about yourself."

"What would you like to know?"

"Well... where do you come from?"

Dhiar grinned broadly down at the man. "You would never in a million years believe me."

"Oh, come on! You know where I'm from!"

"I come from the Abyss," Dhiar replied easily. "See?" And with that, he pointed up to the small horns, exposed by his slicked-back wet hair.

The first impulse for Tomas was to become afraid, but something about Dhiar made him not want to be afraid, nor to be uncomfortable. An instant's tension melted into amusement. "Oh, is that so? It must be a nice place, if there are more like you there. Or did you leave because there weren't?"

"Oh no, there are many like me there. I guess I'm about average." Dhiar laughed deeply again, rubbing along the other man's chest.

"Average!" Tomas nearly choked. His new friend, he felt sure, was many things. "Average" did not number among them.

"Oh, there are plenty of more interesting sorts, I should think. Especially for you." Dhiar ran his first fingertip around the curve of a nipple, bringing it from soft shapelessness to a firm point. "Plenty of better singers and musicians, for one. I dabble, but you know, I'm not really that much of a music-creator, myself..."

Tomas reached up, turning slightly, and found himself face-to-face with Dhiar's rising erection. Swallowing hard, he pulled his eyes away from the sight. He parted his lips, looking up, as if to ask a question that faded before escaping his mouth.

He took the Incubus on his tongue and sank his head down. The taste thrilled him, bringing him to full excitement too. It had been too long, and his body responded to each and every touch and caress.

Dhiar closed his eyes, lips curling up in satisfaction.

Merry and Tomas sat conversing pleasantly, with Chana elbowing Dhiar delicately nearby.

"I don't know how you do it," she mumbled to him, in a tone that only he was likely to hear at all. "You do good, avoiding those jealous spats."

Dhiar just shrugged his shoulders, a wide smile across his face. "I just don't like people getting all hostile over the silliest things. Besides..." he looked down a bit, "I'm still not sure if this place is right for me to settle for any length of time. So if I should have to go again, I've introduced two very special and very interesting people to each other, and maybe... they won't need me, if that happens."

"Berlin?" Chana pouted a bit. "I thought we were going to go and see the cabarets and everything...!"

He raised his hands, holding them before himself and trying to placate her with the gesture. "I still haven't said no! I just want them to have *something*. They've really hit it off. And Merry didn't know too many interesting sorts like Tomas, and Tomas was more or less consumed by his work constantly... so this can only be a good thing for both of them. That's what I think."

"You're probably right."

"I know I am!" He leaned back in his chair, watching the two.

It was an intricate dance, but one he had performed many times. The lingering gazes took it all, with the hesitant, incidental touches punctuating the exchange. He could recall the scents of both of the men, and when he sat with them a moment ago, he felt them mingling. It energised him; the first things to mull and mix about two, when they met, always tended to be the scents. Some formed discordant, clashing substances that made storms from their differences in pressure. Others barely touched each other, held back by diffident aroma almost completely absent. And then there was the perfume between the two he had introduced, only a few minutes after they began to speak. After the hesitance left them, after Dhiar coaxed them into conversation, it became a heady incense.

"I'm going to get another drink. You want one?"

"I'll come with you." Dhiar rose, glancing to the table again. The two didn't even notice him departing. It made him smile again.

"So later I was thinking we're gonna hit the uni and bob for apples in the natatorium, right?"

The Incubus looked at his sister, turning his head slowly to trace her path. "Sorry?"

"The pool! Bobbing for apples! Don't tell me you've never bobbed for apples."

Dhiar started to laugh as he settled up against the bar. It was more a makeshift bar, as the place itself also was more of a makeshift speakeasy, probably ousted from its old foundation and migratory to avoid persecution.

"I can't say I've ever done it in a natatorium," Dhiar replied. "Bobbed for apples, that is."

Chana cracked a grin at the implications of the hasty qualifier.

"Shall we invite the two handsome lads at the table?"

"Tommy and Merry? Yeah!" Chana held up two fingers to the bartender. Two more drinks for them. "The more the merrier! Well, you know what I mean."

Now it was Dhiar's turn, and he raised his voice in laughter at the play on words and Merry's name. All of the partying, the running around, the shopping... the pleasure of Chana's company, all of it had done what she clearly set out to do, and that was to heal Dhiar's pain from Noctemburg. He felt almost completely healed. His heart had made nearly a full recovery.

It seemed so distant, and yet at times it always lingered near. In the night, the darkness held warmth and comfort, but it could also betray with its darkness and pull the curtain back on visions of things that should have slept. The shadows always stretched long in Noctemburg. Here, they either covered the street or barely reached from the walls. Buildings were so close together, in the city.

They collected their drinks and drifted over to the other two and their table.

"So! Gentlemen." Dhiar leaned between them, an arm over each one's shoulders. "We are headed to the natatorium at the uni shortly, bobbing for apples Chana says. Who's up for learning how to use his teeth in the water?"

Both of them laughed and nodded, and Dhiar sat between them at their invitation, with Chana taking the other chair, next to Merry. The conversation never dipped out of the warm realm of comfort and friendship.

It was a short time later that they all found themselves at the university. Naturally, all of this was the work of a fraternity. They quietly gathered at the gates; someone had procured the keys, though no-one entirely knew how. It didn't matter. The doors were opened, the crowd slipped in under the cover of blackest night, and then all was locked again.

Not a single person there had a bathing costume, and so nudity was the order of the day. Wisely, they used the smaller pool, rather than the larger one with the more visible windows. No-one passing outside was likely to detect their presence, even if they made a great sound. Perhaps surprisingly to all, the noise level maintained a decent volume even considering the echo and acoustics.

Dhiar's presence, of course, helped immensely with everything. The men and women playing with apples and each other quickly became more at ease, less frantic and tense, no longer nervous. Everything was nicer, and though more courteous became no less sensual and appealing. Self-conscious modesty sapped away easily, and soon there were easy kisses and happy embraces. The apples bounced in a separate tub of water, and in no short supply, with them taken up and eaten every so often. Naturally, they were full of liquor.

Miraculously, none migrated to the swimming pool. Dhiar sat

dangling his feet into the side of the pool, watching the splashing and horseplay, and some of the sex unfolding in the shallow end, as he munched his latest apple down to its core. He wore not a stitch, legs happily spread, and observed as Chana was carried like the Queen of Sheba on the arms of three naked young polo players to the deep end.

He watched Tomas and Merry cuddling, Tomas's arms around Merry, Merry's head on Tomas's chest. And the two noticed and beckoned him enthusiastically.

Why not? Dhiar tossed his core in the nearby bin and slipped into the water, gliding like a fish through it to them.

42nd Night
Gimme Gimme Gimme

Naked bodies glistened with water and the sparkle of lamps. They hadn't wanted to switch on the electric lights, but they had to provide some illumination in the middle of the night. A Succubus and an Incubus in attendance made it less of a priority for the light to be particularly brilliant; the sense of touch proved much more telling about the geography of the bodies of others.

In short, Dhiar and Chana had completely unintentionally turned the fraternity's natatorium apple-bobbing goof into an impromptu orgy. Everyone seemed to be having quite a good time though, so neither regretted it.

Tomas on one side, dark and mysterious, a siren, and Merry on the other, fair and fragile, both profoundly artistic, pressed against Dhiar. He had introduced them only earlier in the night, and they became fast friends. Now, however, it seemed the whole thing was rising to a new and excitingly different level.

The Incubus could feel both of their bodies, some parts more prominent than others, telling with complete honesty the story of their excitement. Tomas sucked at Dhiar's sensitive earlobe, and the Incubus rose the rest of the way himself. Ears were usually a demon's most erogenous zone, and Dhiar was no exception to this. He let a soft sound escape between his lips, adding to the other ambient noise of pleasure.

A swimming pool transformed into a well of pleasure, in the water and out. It reminded him just a bit of the Pit, the club with the solid water column. He recalled all its thrills and pleasures. His hands slid down the two men's backs, over their buttocks, and then to the hips, before squeezing both in front, wrapping his fingers around and starting to stroke in the water.

Dhiar between the two completed the circuit of ecstasy, and suddenly the mingling of feelings, thoughts, and sensations clicked into place. They had both experienced it with Dhiar, individually, but they now discovered that the presence of additional participants made it even more intense. The waters now hummed with bliss, and they found themselves receiving little snatches of feeling and pulses of arousal from those sharing the pool.

Both slid in concert to make a kind of triangular shape with each of them as one side, and in the middle of it all, three erections pressed heads together. Dhiar took in a slow, shaky breath and pressed hip to hip with the two. And a pair of hands began to stroke and fondle him between his own legs, even as he pumped Tomas and Merry at the same time. It all moved like a well-oiled and intricately-designed machine, yet there was nothing cold or mechanical about it; it moved with purpose and determination, without the slightest amount of doubt between its parts.

If they weren't already in the water, their hands would surely have been dripping by now anyway. Slick, supple skin rubbed against more. Hairs drifted along the body, soft and dreamlike in the water. Three faces drew closer, and three sets of lips explored the others, with a triad of tongues adding to the sensory overload.

Tomas started to go over the edge, which pulled Merry along, and Dhiar shivered as he pushed the both of them with his own empathy. All three simultaneously released in the water, and their bodies needfully pressed against each other. Nothing but hands had produced some of the most amazing of reactions. The sounds they made only encouraged the other participants around them to continue on in whatever they happened to do.

After a short time, they all pulled themselves out of the water. All three bodies, of different sizes and shapes, reclined on the side. Their bodies gleamed and glowed with the after-ecstasy bliss lingering between them. Muscles pulsed with pleasure. The once-furious erections slowly softened, remaining halfway full as their chests rose and fell, catching themselves, calming themselves. In the environment around them, it was no mean feat.

Merry leaned unsurely forward, and Dhiar and Tomas leaned in simultaneously to take half of his lips for theirs. The three-way kiss took his breath away. As it ended, all of them laughed softly, tangling their bodies together as they collapsed to the surprisingly warm tile.

"It's going to be bizarre to put on clothes again," Tomas at last broke the silence.

Dhiar laughed, nodding and rubbing his hand along the small of Merry's back. "It always is, for me. I'm much more comfortable without, but well... sometimes it's nice to parade around in finery like a peacock with feathers you can change."

That reminded him. He glanced over to find Chana, and then hurried his gaze back to the two next to him. His sister was probably the centre of the party. She definitely would not regret this night. She was infused with enough pleasure to last her easily half the year, in this one evening alone.

Merry kissed Dhiar's cheek, then Tomas's, and pushed himself up to his feet, holding his hands out to the two. "Let's get a shower."

"Calling it quits for tonight?" Dhiar hopped to his feet, pulling Tomas up with him.

"It's almost morning!" Merry answered, chuckling and then stretching, arching his back and swinging his arms back. "We'll have to leave soon. Even if it's Sunday, surely we can't be too leisurely or we'll be caught. Let's get a shower and just... linger a little longer."

Tomas nodded energetically, linking arms with the other men and pulling them along to the showers. "A good idea!"

From water to water again they went, sharing a single nozzle of the open showers. There were couples and trios and more using the locker room for whatever purposes they pleased, but the showers, for whatever reason, were for Dhiar and his lovers.

"Let's go back to my place after." Merry lathered Dhiar's chest.

Tomas nodded again, caring for Dhiar's legs. "That sounds good! I'd like to see it."

Meanwhile, Dhiar rapidly rose again. He decided that perhaps the lingering could involve a bit more. Or maybe he could wait until they reached Merry's flat, and Sunday could very well be Funday, all day.

43rd Night
In He Comes

Just for a few weeks. Just a few! Chana had been so very insistent, of course. Dhiar knew he couldn't resist her indefinitely. It was always easier to go along with things, to acquiesce, otherwise she would be inconsolable and utterly torturous to live with for any length of time. He knew what he had to do.

And so Merry and Tomas received their own invitations, but the both of them were content where they were. It was good enough; they could surely get to Berlin easily enough, if they wanted, at some later date. So the Succubus and the Incubus were alone together, again. If they had taken an airplane, it might have been faster. But the both of them loved the romance of the sea, and it would not be all too long that way. They would sail for the first part, and the train would carry them the rest of the way. Perhaps on the return voyage, they would opt for flight.

The launch was stunning, Dhiar reflected; it had been like so many pictures and films, picturesque and breathtaking, stunning too. He waved his handkerchief with a bright smile on his face, as Merry and Tomas, leaning against each other contently, both waved a single hand enthusiastically. He could tell in their eyes that they would miss him. But at the same time, he also knew they would have plenty of good times whilst he hopefully would do the same in the German capital.

Ah, Berlin—if a city ever echoed the sensibilities of his own home, Berlin was it. At least during the 1920s (which this dimension would embrace for ever), it was a place of diversity, the greatest of freedoms in interests. Yet, as with most human endeavours, it remained tinted with a sort of tragedy, a kind of sadness that pervaded the whole place. Even amid the absolute luxury of hedonistic liberation, a darkness settled onto the boughs of the tree.

From what Chana had said, her chronicles of the city painted everything anyone could aspire to have, be, or do, at least on Earth. Her world, her pet world as Dhiar sometimes called it, remained in the "Roaring" era and thrived there. No crash, no impending disaster darkened the horizon. Yet, just as in every other world he knew, things were not always rosy all the time.

Dhiar looked out at the sea, at the waves around them capped and then retreating, rippling in white foam about the cutting shape of the boat tripping through it. He breathed in deeply, inhaling the scent of the open waters, and it made his head swim a bit in vicarious sympathy.

Naturally, the liquor flowed freely on the ship and Chana, once they wandered outside of American waters, decided to drink her fill. Dhiar would join her later. Right now he occupied himself drinking in the soaking air around him.

The ship's rails stood high enough to shield passengers from most of the spray, but he could still feel little droplets cool on his cheeks and forehead. He watched the ship's crew, in smart little suits for their smart tight bodies, as they occupied themselves with the business of sailing. The captain and his first mate, of course, were smartest-attired of all, handsome and well-groomed. Even if their costumery had weathered the rocky seas, they both still possessed the awareness and charm to set most of the passengers swooning.

The first mate wandered over to the Incubus with the captain occupied in a group of ostensibly flappers. He doffed his hat and looked out to the water around them, sidling close to Dhiar with a thin smile. His dimples appeared just so. He couldn't be more than forty, Dhiar mused; perhaps significantly younger, but the long sideburns gave him a look of a man from another time entirely.

"Good day sir. I trust everything is to your satisfaction?"

"Some things more than others!" Dhiar replied, a toothy grin spreading across his face as he leaned closer. "I'm especially interested in the crew, actually."

The man seemed surprised at first, and he chuckled self-consciously before removing his cap completely, resting it against his chest. "Oh? Are you an old sea hand yourself?"

"Let's just say I'm no stranger to seamen," Dhiar replied.

The first mate nearly choked.

Barely any time passed between the conversation at the railside and the subsequent drink. Even if the first mate still technically remained on-duty, it was practically part of that duty that he have a drink with a passenger when invited. Especially those of the echelon of Dhiar and his sister; drinks were complimentary, there; it was practically obligatory for anyone of the crew to bend over backwards, forwards, or whichever way requested... within reason, of course.

But it was within reason as the man sat in the chair next to Dhiar's, raising his glass in a salute to the demon next to him. Both had brightened into even higher spirits than before, and it seemed like a party consisting of two... but two was enough, between them. They chatted and laughed and sipped the delicious wine, and then a mixed drink, a cocktail, a cordial, and at last a bottle of champagne was sat on the centre of their table, in a silver bucket full of ice.

"Really, it's so luxurious," Dhiar purred. He could drink anyone under the table and probably through the floor underneath it, but he was allowing himself to feel a bit of the tingling buzz and comforting numbness washing over his muscles from all the drink. The first mate must have been a hard drinker or gifted supernaturally to remain conscious and as aware as he did.

"So what did you say your name was, sir?" The first mate looked up at Dhiar, his eyes glossy and a bit foggy. It was still to his credit that he remained conscious.

"Dhiar! And you? I can't keep calling you 'first mate', especially if this is going where I think it may be going."

"Adoric," the man answered, chuckling a bit self-consciously and sitting back against the back of his seat.

"Ahh, an appropriate name! Adoric, who is adorable. And dashing. Quite dashing." Dhiar raised his glass again, as if for another sort of toast.

44th Night
Wild Rum

"I'm only doing my job, you understand," Adoric slowly drew in the tobacco smoke into his mouth and throat, and then it filtered out his nose, curling in on itself as he breathed out.

Dhiar held up a hand when offered one of the man's cigarettes, from a silver case engraved with sirens all over it. "Oh no, I couldn't. You're going to need all of them you can get. So," he rolled onto his side. "Your job involves rolls in the hay, as it were, with passengers?"

The first mate rolled to face Dhiar, stroking his cheek with rough fingertips. A man's fingertips who had done so much work with his hands. "Only special ones."

"Such as myself."

"Such as yourself," he echoed, laughing deeply and setting his cigarette down in the ashtray. "Really, I feel a bit like a boy sailor. I am entirely sure I've never jumped into bed with someone so quickly since I said farewell to my teenage years!"

And they lay in bed, facing each other, both naked except for the covers strewn haphazardly around. It looked like the aftermath of a drunken and highly abortive toga party of the inexperienced in Roman fashion of any kind.

Dhiar reached over to the nightstand and took up the man's cap, setting it on the first mate's head and adjusting it to rest at a jaunty angle. "Rakish," he commented, bouncing his brows once.

"I'm told I have a certain rogue appeal." Adoric reached up to right it, eyes shining as he laughed again. "What do you think?" He turned his head from side to side, to present his profile to the Incubus.

Dhiar could only laugh, nodding a couple of times. "Yes, definitely. Not so roguish, in my experience. Just a handsome man of the sea. Sophisticated. Well-read. And may I say, could probably outdrink any living human in the known world. I've never met a human who can drink as much as you can without passing out in his own vomit."

The candor immediately sent Adoric into a fit of giggles, a bit strange-sounding to come from a man with such a deep and full voice. They all danced on the air like little pixies, high-pitched and brightening the air between them.

"No, it's true!" Dhiar immediately added, reaching over to pat the other man's soft-furred chest. "I've never seen anyone who didn't have some sort of supernatural gift put it away like that!"

"Well, I'm a sailor." Adoric at last collected himself enough to say, settling down in the pillows and sheets. "A considerable part of our lives is drinking. And carousing. Except the teetotallers, which I suppose are good for any ship to have."

"I suppose." Dhiar settled down too, resting his head on the fluffy pillow. "Still..."

"You say 'human' as if..."

"As if I'm not one? Well, I'm not." Dhiar pointed to his head, and in specific the small horns in his dark locks. "Incubus. You know. Pleasure demon."

"Oh, I see!" Adoric grinned wider, caressing Dhiar's neck, along his collar, over the centreline of his chest. "That explains a lot. Did you enchant me with some magic spell? Or was it just gravitation?"

"Gravitation cannot be blamed for people falling in love," Dhiar quipped in response, laughing again, in his throat. "Actually, don't quote me on that one." He cleared his throat, a more serious expression coming over his face for only an instant. "I mean, don't quote me on that."

The first mate shook his head and ran his fingers through the hematite curls tumbled over the shoulders of the man before him. "You're so erudite and sophisticated. And so amusing. It's like you've come from another time... you're like nothing and no-one I've ever seen. Anywhere. Ever."

"Thank you!" Dhiar beamed, chest pushing out in pride. "I

take great care to keep my distinctiveness! My people are... well, perhaps unfairly judged, and they've been given especially atrocious reputations, but really we're quite decent."

"I should say so!" Adoric leaned in for a soft kiss, lingering lips upon lips. "So are you going to suck my soul out now?"

"Pff," Dhiar took another kiss after that, nosing the man's cheek. "I've no use for anyone's soul. They're not exactly anything you can trade as a commodity. No, I subsist off pleasure... so it's in my best interests to help others to spread it. To stoke the fire..."

"Fan the flames..."

"Spit alcohol into them when necessary," Dhiar finished, laughing in time with Adoric.

The two let their hands slowly wander, across hair and hairless regions, in the depths and at the surface, in each and every crevasse and out of it, the sides of the valleys and the rolling incline of the peaks. Their bodies responded to every touch; Dhiar's closeness made it all seem so much more urgent and frantic than it otherwise would. There was so much depth in every move, every slightest thing that they shared.

Adoric rolled atop Dhiar and the two began to grind, each growing firmer between the legs easily and quickly. The Incubus closed his legs and moved carefully, flexible like a gymnast, taking the first mate's hardness between his thighs. It had been so long— so long!—since Adoric had even so much as proposed such an intercourse with anyone. But he had wanted it, and now he had it; the last time he remembered between the thighs was with a French prostitute, or a prostitute who spoke some French and had some French affectations. She was nice. He would have to pay her a call next time he came to her port.

But all thoughts of Paris Mary fled from his mind after that instant. He could feel he was dripping, leaking sticky and slick between the firmly-pressed thighs, matting hair and pushing it down and up and every direction.

"It's all right, let it go." Dhiar looked up into his eyes, and in that instant Adoric felt his whole body wash over with ecstasy and bliss. It was like nothing else. It reminded him of being pulled down by the undercurrent. He could see no surface in reach.

And then he let go.

45th Night
Meteor

"So what's your hometown like?"

"You'd like it," Dhiar answered, leaning against Adoric under the stars, on the deck. The chill in the air and the sea spray had driven all the rest of the passengers inside. "It's on the water."

"Really! Actually I'm from a landlocked place." The first mate exhaled a cloud of smoke that drifted out around his head like a halo. "I always wanted to see the sea, sail the oceans. I read all the stories about Sindbad and you know... all of his adventures, his ordeals..."

The Incubus turned his head to kiss softly at the place where the man's ear met his cheek. He lowered his voice, deep and intimate. "And have you had adventures and ordeals like Sindbad?"

Adoric's cheeks reddened, and a shiver ran down his back. "A few."

"Tell me."

"But you're a demon! I mean... you must have had far more exciting adventures than I..."

"No, no. Tell me." Dhiar reached over to stroke the man's chest, through the turtleneck he wore. "I'm interested in you."

The blush on the man's cheeks deepened, and he looked down at the glowing cherry of his cigarette. "Well... it was some time ago. It's been smooth sailing on this liner. Not so much to do with passenger cruises, but when I wasn't on this ship... things were different!"

He took another draw from the cigarette. "I remember one of the ships, it was barely seaworthy, hardly ship-shape. The men were a potpourri, a patchwork quilt made from the oddest variety of ports. I was always the captain's favourite, but that was probably as much my capability as my looks, to be honest with you. He never seemed to carouse too much when we went to port, but I knew how he looked at me wasn't the way a man looks at another unless he has a sort of interest in him."

"Like this?" Dhiar flared his eyes open and made a mock-intense stare, and the both of them broke into laughter.

"Not quite! But something like that. Not too different... anyway, in those days I was less earnest and far less dutiful. It was a different time, a different place..."

"Many different places," Dhiar chimed in.

"Right! But I remember once, when we went inland... oh, it was atrocious. One of the crew was this grubby little man, always looking for something shiny. And that in and of itself isn't so bad. Everyone wants a little treasure. I think every sailor took his first step aboard a ship because there was the promise of treasure. It's a bit like life, if I might be so bold as to philosophise; taking the first steps because, somewhere beyond our sight and just out of our grasp, the promise exists of something shining and brilliant that we can hold as our own."

He looked up to the Moon, which looked benevolently over them, clouds curled around it in the air with glitter-stars on the firmament surrounding. "There was a little church in the town, and we didn't think much about it. But apparently they were highly influential... and the little blighter stole some icon from them. It was just a little thing... but it was as if the entire town had been turned, zombie-like, against us. There were accusations, counter-accusations, and we found ourselves at the business end of several unpleasant-looking weapons, bladed and blunt."

"My goodness!"

"But we weren't about to get ourselves locked up, and they weren't about to listen. None of us knew the little fellow had done what he had done, and it wasn't a port we frequented. We had never really been there before, we'd only heard stories. But we were to find that it was hardly a place we should have stopped, regardless of its convenience."

"You couldn't have known, of course!"

"Of course not, but it was still a mad time. Madness!" Adoric shook his head slowly. "We barely got out intact, barely with our skins! I thought it would be the last port we would land... but it turned out to be just another adventure. I'm glad we came out alive, though I'm not proud to say I had to take a few of the weapons and turn them on their owners. Non-lethally, of course; I'm sure they had some nasty headaches."

He took a breath in, then sighed and settled against Dhiar, pressing the remainder of his cigarette into the thick green glass ashtray. "We tried to explain, but they wouldn't hear it. We honestly ended up tossing the damned thing off the boat as we were pulling out to sail, and they scrambled for it like a bunch of seagulls for a piece of bread. Or ants for a sugar cube. It was... almost inhuman, how they did. Their eyes were so glassy and hollow..."

"You might've stumbled upon something more than just humans at a place. Perhaps it was a cursed locale, or perhaps another presence there influenced them."

"There are more things in this world than I understand, or ever will." Adoric slipped his fingers between Dhiar's and squeezed his hand tenderly. "I was just happy to get away from the place. We never went back."

"And the little fellow?"

"Booted out on the next port. The captain threatened to throw him to the place we'd just barely escaped." Adoric laughed loudly, echoing in his chest. "He was a bit of a bastard though, so none of us were too sad to see him go. Awful man. I don't mind picking up a bit of treasure here and there, but one must be prudent..."

"Yes, about what one chooses to take! Sometimes it's something that will set off a whole town into a murderous rage, apparently."

"I'm glad I got out of it."

"Tell me more." Dhiar reached up to turn the man's chin toward him, looking deep into his eyes. "I want to know everything, especially everything you've felt you could never share with anyone else."

"You've already shared so much with me," Adoric replied, leaning his head closer. "I'll share all I can with you."

46th Night
Universe Tipping

"I come from a city on the water," Dhiar explained, his voice sweet and lingering on the air, vibrating lightly in the ears. "Tall and short buildings, stone paths all around, winding between the buildings and neighborhoods. So many trees. The grandest trees dwarf all the buildings, making huge canopies. Their arms stretch out, as if they were our guardians. They may well be."

Adoric's eyes were wide. He lifted his arms as the Incubus slipped his shirt off after his turtleneck. The man's body felt warm and soft, with the light hairs all over the chest and down to the navel. He eased back to the bed, atop the mattress, and Dhiar all but draped over him like a personal blanket.

"There are cathedrals of tea and dance halls where a solid column of water lets you fly without leaving it. The music pulses through your body and moves you even if you stand still. You can close your eyes and float for ever."

The first mate's eyes closed. Dhiar worked his trousers down.

"Sometimes they play the most wonderful songs. They encourage one to stop, in every sense, and relax as much as possible. It's a deep relaxation, right down to the soul. The body tingles and even becomes a little numb. You can see all the colours with your eyes closed... colours that wouldn't exist elsewhere, colours that don't exist in any other world. I've never seen them elsewhere, even with my eyes closed."

Dhiar's hand stroked along the curve of the man's chest, over a nipple that too quickly rose to firmness. "And there's a hall of portals, opened to places countless, with a million doors at least. Some open to other doors. Some merely look onto worlds with windows. There are a thousand little rounded halls to look out and step from the city."

"How do you return?" Adoric's eyes opened again, to look up at the Incubus as he undressed himself.

"You... sort-of find the door again," Dhiar hesitated only for a moment. "It's a bit tricky to describe in words, but you know it's there. It's easy to find, you just have to..." he gesticulated vaguely, "feel it."

"Feel it." The man echoed, sliding his hands to catch at Dhiar's waist and unfastening his trousers. He worked them over the Incubus's hips, down over his buttocks, over his thighs, and down along his calves.

"Mm." Dhiar dipped his head for a soft kiss. "And mountains all around. And trains. There are plumes like elegant little chimney-stacks with wheels, coming and going. You can take a train to everywhere, where I'm from. And everyone loves it. It's the most luxurious and pleasing experience. There are trains all over. Sometimes one just boards a train for fun, or relaxation, or pleasure."

"When I was a boy," Adoric murmured, "I also dreamed, when I was very young mind you, about being the conductor of a train. But ships were my true love, I found, when I first boarded one. My sea-legs are stronger than my land-legs."

"But have you ever boarded a train, to try?" Dhiar's mouth spread into a grin, showing his brilliant teeth. "Perhaps that would get your land-legs stronger."

"Well," Adoric looked away, thinking, "I've ridden trains, of course. Who hasn't?"

"But have you boarded a train to pilot it? To be a conductor?"

"No, never."

"Maybe you ought to try, sometime." Dhiar lowered his lips to the man's chest, kissing down the centre, then to either side, one at a time, over nipple and hair and stocky muscle, down over the ribs and to the centre again of the chest, down to the navel, then slowly below.

"I wouldn't know where to start."

"Start at the beginning," Dhiar ran his hands over Adoric's stomach and out along the sides, pulling back to his hips and holding them, looking up at him. He could feel the arousal below, but it was a lazy one, still hot and fragrant.

"That seems redundant," Adoric snorted, but he grinned by the end of it.

"No, no. Many people want to run before they can walk. You could at least read a book on it or something."

"When I was a boy, I suppose I read a few books..."

"On trains?"

"Right, I mean, that's what I mean!" He laughed and pushed a hand through Dhiar's curls. "I'm not running before I can walk. But I'd need training and such."

"You didn't become a first mate by being unable to learn."

"No, you're right." Adoric tickled his fingers softly at the base of Dhiar's neck. "Perhaps one day I'll follow that dream."

"It needn't be now, or soon." Dhiar kissed at Adoric's stomach, then down, down past the dark and soft fluff of hairs, then onto the rising arousal. "We're occupied at the moment anyway."

"Ah, yes." The first mate kept petting Dhiar's hair, kneading his scalp, raising his hips and rocking at the tongue and lips attending him. "It's so good."

The Incubus dispensed with words, then, and let one hand wander down at the weighty orbs hanging between the man's legs. His velvet sac tightened towards his body again in excitement, as his member stood full upright at attention in barely a handful of seconds.

"So... very good..."

Adoric's thoughts were like a tornado, frantic and quick and full of so many different things. He could scarcely concentrate, but the overbearing quality within his mind was Dhiar, everything Dhiar. The Incubus had made him fall in love and dominated his thoughts... but it was a natural thing, not coercion or intimidation. It was the happiest he had ever felt, possibly even happier than that first voyage, the thrill that caught in his throat when the ropes were loosed and the ship swayed and rocked with the rhythm of the waters.

He felt this port to be his own, this magnificent and welcoming place of rest. Though like any port, he could never own it, he knew it would always bear him safely home.

47th Night
Trouble Me

Dhiar slid his hands up Adoric's tunic, feeling the hair on his chest and over his stomach. He sighed and kissed at the back of the man's neck. Chana was well on her way to take the train. She'd be in Berlin days or weeks before he would be, but he resolved he could not leave Adoric so quickly.

The first mate, meanwhile, had requested some leave and of course got it; he was actually more senior than the current captain of the vessel.

"So, shall we get off to the north? Perhaps the Isle of Man?"

Dhiar grinned just a tad more at that suggestion. "You really do have a keen sense of humor. No-one else would ever suggest that to me."

Adoric chuckled, leaning back against the Incubus. "Of course, I doubt we'll get underway if you keep that up."

"It was nice of them to let you hire a ship for nothing." Dhiar seemed to ignore the little tease entirely.

"For what I've done? Pish-posh. It'll be brought back in better condition than it's seen for years." The first mate breathed deeply in, reaching back to squeeze Dhiar's buttock.

The Incubus responded instantly by grinding against the sailor's backside. "So," he rumbled, full of smouldering desire, "Scotland?"

Adoric nodded once, squeezing again before pulling away. He turned around, to face Dhiar, and leaned in for a quick but deep kiss. "There. I've a friend up there. We'll sail up and impose on his hospitality a little."

"Excellent." Dhiar rested his arms on Adoric's shoulders. "What can I do in the meantime?"

"It won't be much to get this ship up there," the first mate replied, walking around the deck to pull at some of the riggings, making sure they were secure. "This time of year, we can probably keep the engines at a minimum. The route I have in mind should allow us to use sails a good amount of the time."

Dhiar kept close behind, leaning down and over, here and there, to inspect after the man had led the way. "It's very desirable, you know, to see a man who knows what he's doing."

"Or at least gives that impression?" Adoric turned, his grin spreading. "Don't worry. I really do know a thing or two about running a ship."

"It's a cosy little craft!" Dhiar clasped his hands together, hurrying to the sailor's side. "Shall we get underway?"

"Let's! At this rate, it won't take us more than a few hours if we keep to the routes I know." The first mate motioned to the ropes across from him. "Take those and... I presume you know how to do what I'm about to ask you to do?"

Dhiar answered with a nod, going to the ropes immediately. "I didn't grow up on a ship, but I've been around so many that I'm sure I can handle one." He lowered his voice, a playful tone coming to it. "I certainly can handle sailors."

"You certainly can!" A laugh, and then the sail unfurled, and the two set about keeping it in place.

A few more preparations, and then the boat swayed onto the waves and northward. The weather continued pleasantly enough, but the latitude alone meant that the journey swiftly turned chill. A few jaunts through misty, freezing rain and fog made it seem almost like sailing into another world, but both of them knew all too well that they had not left the one of their journey's origin.

The stretch became steady and straightforward, so they retreated to the cabin. Adoric kept the wheel, leaning his arms lazily on it and practically draping his whole body across it. Dhiar nursed another cup of coffee; it had kept the both of them going since they left port. Even though the quarters were cramped, the small kitchen space allowed for a tiny stove and just enough room for hot drinks.

"Another cup for you?" The Incubus called, pausing with the special pot made to resist messy sloshing.

"I'd... better not." Adoric glanced over his shoulder, with an apologetic flash of a grin.

Dhiar's brows raised. "Oh?" He sipped his own beverage. "Why not?"

The sailor cleared his throat, looking back to the front. "No reason," he tried, at first. But after a few seconds, he shook his head, cheeks colouring. "When I was still a green deck hand, I used to live off coffee," he explained, motioning with one hand, the other still draped on the wooden wheel. "Until one day, when I made an important discovery. You see, there's a head on board most every ship. A toilet, you know."

Dhiar nodded his head, leaning against the wall.

"And usually the work is so that you sweat it out anyway, or you're on deck and can just take a moment away and give back to the sea, well... this time it wasn't quite like that. Too much to do on-deck, but not enough to keep me from needing relief."

It dawned, then, on Dhiar, and he kept himself from giggling. The image in his mind really charmed him. "At least you were on-deck, though. I'm sure the waves helped you."

Adoric laughed, instead, shaking his head. "I was too far back, holding the rope while another crewman took his sweet time doing something else, I forget what. The captain, I'm sorry to say, never let me forget about it, though he and everyone else were fairly kind overall."

Dhiar looked into his coffee, the scene lively in his mind's eye. He absently wished he could have been there. How cute, how endearing... how sensual! It excited him, more than a little bit. It was Adoric, after all, and little that he ever did could dissuade the Incubus from his pursuit and his affections.

"So should we venture outside and make sure the ropes are fast, and return a little water to the ocean?" Dhiar wandered to the sailor's side, looking out through the windows that opened to the sea before them. "The fish'll like it. It's caffeinated."

Adoric swatted Dhiar's ass, shaking his head, the grin still persistent on his face. "I can't just let the ship try to steer itself for any length of time. I'm stuck in here, which is why I ought not to drink much of that brew."

"Ah." Dhiar leaned against his side. "Well, in that case, if you're staying in... so am I."

The first mate grinned again, showing all his bright teeth, looking to the Incubus at his side. "Is this a contest?"

"Maybe."

48th Night
Dry Grass and Shadows

Here they were, more than halfway to Scotland, and the two of them bounced impatiently in the cabin of the ship. The sun drew closer to the horizon, and soon the sky would be illuminated only by the pinpricks of stars and the distant glow of the occasional port town.

Dhiar could have just altered his body, but that wouldn't have been sporting. Besides which, he had reached and surpassed the point where any significant alterations of the body were only reluctantly undertaken; Chana seemed to have more proclivities to shapeshifting than he did. He felt it was just an unnecessary bother, aside from the occasional detail, here or there.

And as such, he knew that this was a challenge he stood a good chance of losing. But due to his empathic abilities, he also could feel Adoric's own desperate attempts to keep his control. They had already gone drinking with each other, enough to drink anyone else under the table. Both had kept their composure, neither had humiliated himself. This time might be different.

"Another shot?" Dhiar held up the bottle of scotch. It was reasonable, since they were headed to Scotland, after all. As if the coffee weren't enough!

The sailor cleared his throat and threw his shoulders back, lifted his chin, and motioned to the Incubus. "If you'll have one."

It had been challenge after challenge. Of course Dhiar would have to take a drink too. Otherwise, it wouldn't be fair. Given, Dhiar had enjoyed more coffee than Adoric, but there were certain advantages that the demon held. Adoric considered it not an unfair thing if they kept even from the moment the challenge was recognised.

And anyway, he wasn't too worried about winning or losing. He hadn't confessed it to Dhiar, but it excited him a bit. The earlier experience had not been at all unpleasant: a relief, and warm, and almost like an orgasm as it shot through his body. A little thrilling. Certainly forbidden, and coming from that cock he liked so much... well, perhaps being around Dhiar made him a bit more adventurous than usual. He might not have considered it with another partner, but with Dhiar... the Incubus surely would be able to appreciate the sensual aspects of it. It was only natural, after all, and came from a man.

His eyes fixated on Dhiar's crotch as the Incubus adjusted his trousers. He could see the familiar shape behind the cloth, and he could tell it was slightly full. A little excited, just a bit. Just like his own, which he was sure Dhiar could tell. It seemed the demon could just glance at a man and penetrate the entirety of his attire to see him, naked and defenceless.

Both men lifted their shot glasses, and both took the drink of scotch. It burned the throat, made it tingle, but by now it was hardly such a considerable burn. The both of them were quite experienced in drinking great quantities of alcohol.

The best part of scotch was absent in many other forms, and that was the phenomenon of "whiskey dick"; that is to say, the tingling warmth that tickled at the tip of the penis. Adoric breathed in and reflected that perhaps that was what brought him back every time to the drink. Even on the loneliest night, it always gave him a thrill. If he drank it quickly enough, he could slip into a deep sleep and dream of the pleasures he had not experienced for some time, until meeting Dhiar.

On all of the charts, he could not plot out where he thought Dhiar had come from. He knew it could not be anywhere as mundane as his own hometown, or any other he had seen in his travels. He wondered exactly where Dhiar's home lay on the maps. He had spoken so majestically about it; the sailor wanted to pilot the boat there and see it. But he imagined one day, he probably would.

Both glasses slammed onto the wooden surface. Dhiar hiccuped, and Adoric laughed at the sound. He immediately wished he hadn't. That just made it all the more difficult.

But then he felt Dhiar's hand on his crotch, and his eyes met the Incubus's, and he felt the demon's lips on his own and his warmth and fragrance so close.

"I will if you will," he murmured, voice a temptation greater than the mists of opium from a den, or the open thighs of easy virtue.

Whether it was the drink they had tossed carelessly down, or the coffee before, or the intoxicating nearness of the Incubus, Adoric leaned right into the hand and laughed again, this time fully aware of what it would bring.

And it did bring that very thing, warmth and wetness mingling between them and especially over Dhiar's fingers and palm. He kneaded as he rubbed his palm at the sailor's crotch and relaxed himself.

There was something about the mingling between their shoes, two little ponds merging to form a sea of sorts, an ocean of their desire, and the pleasure-enhancing aura of the Incubus only made it into that much more intense an experience. With the touching, the nearness, and the enhanced sensations, Adoric came despite himself and felt a stickiness join the damp warmth. On the chilly night, it was welcome.

After all was said and done, Dhiar licked up to Adoric's lips and then pushed him against the wall, kissing him harder than he had ever done. He found himself responding, grinding up against the Incubus. It thrilled him in the most forbidden of ways. He knew he shouldn't feel so aroused or excited by it, but with Dhiar, who could help himself? Even only a short time after having lost his own orgasm, he felt his cock filling again.

"I have an idea," Dhiar murmured in his ear, before nibbling the lobe. "Let's take off all our clothes and go out on deck and let the waves wash us clean."

Adoric was naked before another minute passed, and with his penis bobbing eagerly before him, he danced naked on the deck with the unclothed Incubus.

49th Night
Carnival

Two bodies writhed, wet and supple, on the deck.

At first it had started with getting clean. That lasted an impressive handful of seconds before the sheer lust of seeing the naked body of lovers overtook them; it was remarkable, actually, that they had lasted this long without entering one or the other.

It seemed more as if the both of them desired the other so much that they could not co-ordinate it easily; one would wrap his legs around the other and roll underneath, but the rubbing and grinding only continued. It was difficult to ascertain exactly how much of the wetness on them was the waves, how much was precum, and how much had existed there before, from their little contest in the cabin.

All the hair on their bodies matted against their skin, one figure pinker than the other, who was hairier, they wrestled and rolled from side to side. Each one sported a proud, erect penis, and they clapped against each other with every slightest movement. At times, it almost seemed miraculous that they remained in more or less the same spot on the deck. It was fortunate, too, that their sailing stretch kept straight and true.

No words passed between their lips; they were too busy to form any sort of verbal communications. Tongues flicked out every so often, but only when their mouths dared to wander too far from each other. Even without venturing too far into each other, the men gave an impression of almost inseparable closeness.

A mist descended upon the ship and the water, and it made their muscles glisten and gleam more than they did already. Buttocks flexed, thighs tensed, and the faintest glimpse of an anus tightened, framed by hairs glistening wetly in the darkening evening. The sun had almost disappeared beyond the horizon now. The night would be upon them, and then surely they would need to focus on their destination.

Sweat disappeared, rolling down the supple bodies with the splash of mist and water from the sea. Adoric drove his point home and fucked Dhiar soundly for a few slapping seconds, but then with a roll the situation reversed itself, and he found himself being slammed into. It didn't matter, of course; Dhiar's unique gift meant that either way, he experienced all of it and enjoyed every second.

That was another thing that constantly ran through the man's mind. Others he would have doubted, but not Dhiar. The Incubus surely, unquestionably had gifts that anyone else would have given everything to possess. He had never experienced such bliss, such ecstasy, and even when he himself had done nothing directly. It made the sailor want to try everything, no matter how taboo or unthinkable. If it could bring any sort of pleasure, it could be enhanced by Dhiar and made into a sublime rapture.

It improved sex. He always preferred the build-up, the foreplay, and all the sensual interactions. The climax was good, but that was a goal, a point to build to; after it was achieved, that was all. With Dhiar, foreplay was as good as the finish, if not better. It suddenly ceased to matter much if he actually released physically during their lovemaking. Touches, kisses, strokes, and caresses gave him exactly the same pleasures. He often found himself uncontrollably ejaculating several times over the course of a night with Dhiar.

And Dhiar, meanwhile, loved every bit of it. A partner like Adoric was rare, he had found, one who could keep going even after losing it time and again. Wet and sticky for little bursts, he knew it would not take away from the fun. He continued to grapple, like some sort of ancient Greek wrestling match, on the deck. He could feel the slats of wood under his back, then under his hands, as the two of them rolled for supremacy.

Adoric caught the demon's cock with his thighs, and Dhiar thrusted between the muscular, hair-covered legs. The waves of pleasure crashed between them, with the real water smashing against the ship's hull and sending spray of salty water over the both of them.

The two men's lips locked again in kisses that locked out everything else. A pair of tongues, one sharper and rougher than the other, intertwined and lapped, teased at one another. One chest hairy and solid, the other lean and smooth and toned, rubbed against each other. Two erections, gently curved, locked with one another and pulled back, then pressed against two stomachs.

Thunder rumbled in the distance, but lightning never flashed across the sky. The two men seemed to mingle and lose each one in the other. At last, Dhiar cried out, and Adoric groaned, though both sounds were swallowed by the sea and its energetic rush. A greater wave poured over them, washing them clean from the nectar they had shared just a moment before, and the Incubus laughed, helping up his sailor friend.

The two scrambled, naked as before, to pilot the ship and secure the sails. It was not a proper storm, but if unattended it could wreck the ship. And so, without a stitch of clothing, they piloted the boat through the turbulence, thrill pulsing through both as they glimpsed the other, naked and fit and gleaming in the fury of nature, as it was meant to be, as it was natural. The form as nature had crafted and intended showed itself against the occasional and sudden shower of rain.

Just as soon as it had begun, the little storm dissipated. Dhiar flung himself along Adoric's side, laughing and resting his head on the man's shoulder. The two stood naked at the wheel, steering the ship to port. The people in the town, if they caught a glimpse of the two, would probably laugh to themselves: two men without clothes on, bringing the boat to moor.

But the late hour made the docks a scantly-populated place. Only a few salty sailors milled about, and only a couple of them spared a glance to the incoming ship. Not one commented on it, though. When one was out at sea, any port in a storm...!

"My dear sailor," Dhiar murmured, kissing at Adoric's cheek. "I look forward to this lovely holiday with you."

"If it's anything as it's begun so far, I know I'll have the time of my life!" Adoric turned and lifted Dhiar into the air, then set him down and kissed his lips soundly.

50th Night
Is That All There Is?

"So what happened to Adoric?" Joshua looked up from eating his soup. "And what happened in Berlin?"

Dhiar waved a hand. "I've been boring you with my reminiscing for long enough. Are you sure that's enough for you to eat? I can whip up another pot of it in no time..."

The young werewolf laughed, sitting back. "It's fine! You're going to make me fat."

"You could use a little weight!" The Incubus countered, reaching over to ruffle Joshua's bushy hair.

He was right, of course. When he had come to Phantasies, Joshua had been all but skin and bones. It was still easy to see his ribs, each and every one. But slowly, surely, Dhiar's storytelling and cooking had filled him out a bit. He no longer looked like a sad stray, but more a fit young man who simply needed some recovery from a bad stretch.

Joshua finished his bread and tipped the bowl of soup to his lips, draining it dry. He licked his lips and then wiped his mouth with the napkin on the table.

Dhiar rose and collected the dishes, smiling pleasantly, satisfied at what he saw. Little by little, he could tell things were looking up. He set everything in the sink and took a cloth to wipe up the table, then offered his hand to Joshua. The young werewolf took it and rose, and the both of them migrated to the living room.

"Chana phoned yesterday." Dhiar lowered himself onto the sofa, Joshua curling against his side to listen. "She'll be back shortly. She was saying something about television advertisement, but I think the shop does just fine. What do you think?"

Joshua looked up with wide eyes, as if the direct question had caught him off his guard. He shook his head and rolled his shoulders back. "It can't hurt, right?"

The Incubus leaned over and nuzzled at the top of Joshua's hair, breathing slowly in, breathing his scent. It was fresh now, since he regularly washed and made himself at home in the loft. But that virile aroma, the personal perfume, was still palpable to one with as keen senses as Dhiar. His eyes closed. He slipped his arms around Joshua and pulled him closer, lying back and settling horizontally on the cushions with the younger man.

"So what did happen? Why isn't Adoric with you here?" Joshua's gaze remained clear, his expression earnest. There was no guile to be found in his countenance.

It amused Dhiar. That aspect was a strong and rare one they had in common.

"So many things! I can't possibly tell you all of them in just the time the evening has left. I'd rather spend it with you, and now." The Incubus combed his fingers through the lush hair. It had been a dark reddish-brown the first time they met each other, but somehow it had lightened since then. Perhaps, he reflected, his shampoo or oil might have affected such a change. "But if you insist..."

Joshua made a little sound, like a whimper, and rubbed his cheek against Dhiar's.

"Oh, I can't resist that!" And so Dhiar propped his forehead against Joshua's. He let his hands wander up and down the young man's back, body pressed against his own. "All right. Well. Let me see... I can summarise it for you, all right? And then we've got to get on with tonight, and I can tell you in detail later."

The werewolf laughed and pulled back, eagerly nodding his head, then leaning back in. "Tell me! I want to know."

That his adventures had been so compelling satisfied Dhiar. At the time, he only viewed them as fun, or adventure, certainly nothing exceptional for any sort of audience. But ever since he took Joshua in, every night unfolded much the same: stories, dinner, more stories, a bath, then a story before bed.

"Well, Adoric and I spent plenty of fun time together... many, many adventures. I should think he's probably still bouncing about Europe, from what we discussed, that last time..." Dhiar took a breath and softly sighed, thinking back. "Oh, it was wonderful. He's wonderful. I really ought to get back to him and peek in, see what he's doing..."

"Yes! I'd love to meet him!" Joshua bounced, draping his arms over Dhiar and hugging about him.

"We can go sometime soon." Dhiar lightly kneaded with his fingertips at the back of Joshua's scalp. "Mm, but you have to get your strength fully back, first. There's plenty of magic in that place, around that time... that world is dripping with it. You might be overwhelmed if you're not at your best and strongest."

"I promise!"

"When I caught up with Chana in Berlin, it was just splendid. There's everything in that city. It's not all good, but it's certainly not bad. There's a sort of balance struck at that time, and it keeps going, giving and taking endlessly. It's like a sort of yin-yang thing. There's some danger, of course. There are other things in that city, things that are hard to describe to you. But it was an exciting trip. I'm glad I went. I'm glad she talked me into it."

Joshua nodded happily. "Did you go back after and see Merry and everyone?"

"Oh yes! Yes, I spent some significant time with Merry and Tomas. They were together, by the time I left again."

"I do like a happy ending." Joshua tucked his head down to rest against Dhiar's chest.

"Me too." Dhiar kissed the top of the werewolf's head and closed his eyes. His fingertips danced along the bare shoulders, the smooth skin, and he shared his warmth. Outside, it was beginning to get a chill in the air.

The clouds faintly glowed with the last remnants of the sunset. The days had grown shorter too. A few people milled along the street outside. And when the rest of the lights went out, the familiar warm glow smiled out from the oriel window.

About the Author

From an early age, Hushicho held a special passion for storytelling. Throughout his life, he has worked in numerous media and various places in the world. Currently his medium of choice is that of sequential art, or comics, and *Incubus Tales* has the distinction of being the longest-running comic of its type still running. He maintains an international readership and is active promoting environmental awareness and opposing censorship. Another of his passions is cooking and spreading the love of delicious vegetarian fare. Hushicho currently resides in the United States.

more titles you may enjoy from Circlet Press!

The Drag Queen of Elfland by Lawrence Schimel
The Drag Queen of Elfland is a collection of fantastical stories imbued with a refreshingly queer sensibility. These seventeen stories feature a lesbian werewolf taking back the night, a gay vampire discovering the perils of going to the gym (too many mirrors, for starters), a young lord's son undertaking a quest to obtain a magical sword and win the heart of the boy he loves, and much more. Sometimes funny, sometimes moving, sometimes sexy, and always imaginative, these stories show readers the secret worlds that lurk beneath the surface of our own.

Wired Hard 5 edited by Joy Crelin
This fifth volume in Circlet Press's Wired Hard anthology series collects five stories exploring gay male sexuality and themes of isolation and connection through the lens of erotic science fiction and fantasy. Wired Hard 5 includes stories by Jonathan Hepburn, Hero Freyr, Benji Bright, Laylah Hunter, and Sasha Payne.

Extraordinary Deviations: Transgender Erotica by Raven Kaldera
The common conception of gender is turned on its head in these eight sensual stories by long-time Circlet author Raven Kaldera. From the ancient Roman Empire to the future to fantasy worlds, these stories follow people in their exciting and often kinky erotic adventures beyond the gender binary.

more titles you may enjoy from Circlet Press!

Blood Kiss:Vampire Erotica edited by Cecilia Tan
The vampire has always been viewed as a sensual creature. They are hunters and seducers of their prey, the hunt as primal and animal as sex itself. They are outside of the strictures of "common" propriety, the chastity of marriage broken, the purity of the virgin defiled. In these seven seductive tales, sex and death and eternal life are intertwined as vampires of all descriptions—men and women and otherwise, gay and straight and bisexual—come together for danger-laced erotic encounters with humans and with each other.

Fantastic Erotica:The Best of Circlet Press 2008-2012
To celebrate the 20th Anniversary of Circlet Press, Fantastic Erotica presents the very best erotic science fiction and fantasy short stories published by Circlet in the past five years. Chosen by popular vote by the readership from among all the stories published by Circlet from 2008 to the present, these favorites are the cream of the crop.

Scheherazade's Façade edited by Michael M. Jones
The gender lines are blurred and transcended in twelve tales of magic, self-discovery, and adventure, penned by some of today's most intriguing authors. In these pages, you'll find heroes and villains, warriors and tricksters, drag queens and cross-dressers, tragedy and triumph. Featuring all-new work from Tanith Lee, Sarah Rees Brennan, Alma Alexander, Aliette de Bodard, and more.